Alchemy and Argent

MODERN MAGICK, 9

CHARLOTTE E. ENGLISH

1

'Cordelia Vesper,' said Valerie, in the resonant tone of a disapproving headmistress. 'You are bored.'

'I deny it,' I said instantly.

Val looked pointedly at my desk, and all the evidence to the contrary strewn across it. I'd adopted an out-of-the-way nook in the library at Home, tucked under one of the big, bright windows overlooking the sun-baked grounds. The window was wide open, letting in all the intense heat of mid-August and an occasional, desultory stir of air. Not enough of a breeze to cool me down. More than enough to cause havoc among the thousand or so sweet wrappers littering my desk top.

'I got hungry,' I said, as a faint puff of wind whisked a few more onto the floor.

Val folded her arms. Ordinarily stationed at her enormous desk at the entrance to the library — where she was on guard as much as on duty, nobody touched Val's books without permission and expected to get away with it — she had floated through in her imposing green velvet chair to come check on me.

If only she could have done so back when I'd still been industriously employed. Like, about three days ago.

I gazed back at her innocently, and thumped the top of my respectable-looking stack of books. 'Lots of good stuff happening.'

'Excess of sweets,' said Val, pointing. 'Dearth of notes. Phone. *Far* too much staring out of the window. Need I go on?'

She was right on all points. My notebook, optimistically opened at a clean page, had exactly three words written in it ("Nicolas Flamel sucks"). My phone lay on top, screen on, currently displaying an ongoing text conversation between me and Alban that had not, to my regret, received any new instalments since Monday.

And I *had* been staring out of the window. It was the heat that did it, I swear. I wore the airiest summer dress I possessed (pale blue silk), and my hair (silver this week) was scraped up off my neck, but nothing could keep me cool in thirty-four degree heat. Not even in the great stone pile that is Home.

I drooped in my chair. Busted. 'All right, all right. I'm bored out of my skull. It's been two and a half weeks, Val.'

Her brows rose. *She* looked cool as a proverbial cucumber, her dark skin free of the perspiration so unbecomingly glimmering upon my own, her black hair elegantly swept up and frizz-free. Is there a charm to keep cool in summer? Why hasn't anyone ever told me? 'Whatever happened to Library Fiend Ves?' said she.

She had a point. The old me would never have got bored in a library like this. What was *wrong* with me.

I opened my mouth to defend myself, came up with nothing, and shut it again. 'I'm the worst person alive,' I said instead. 'All that time complaining that I wanted to come Home, and now look at me. *Bored.*'

Val softened. 'It is understandable. After weeks on end of wild adventures and daring deeds, the change of pace has been abrupt.'

Maybe that was it. Out on the Fifth Britain, chasing down the clues we need to halt the decline of magick, I'd felt like I was really doing something. Something *important.*

It was harder to feel the same way about combing through dusty old books, considering that the vast majority proved to have nothing useful in them at all.

'I'm addicted to danger,' I sighed. 'Hooked on adventure. The new Ves needs peril and adversity to thrive.'

'I think you were getting tired of that, too,' Val justly observed.

'You're right. Nothing pleases me. I've become a monster.'

She grinned. 'Why don't you take a break?'

'Nooooo.' I sat up, wielding my pen with intent.

'Why not?'

'This *is* an important job, and we haven't made much progress on it. I just need to focus.' All this started a few weeks back, when Val uncovered no fewer than *two* ancient alchemists — self-professed — who claimed to have performed wonders regarding *ordinarie metals such as sylver or gould given magycke beyond their common bounds*. Sounds promising, no? But one turned out to be about as magickal as a lump of plastic; his books were essentially fiction. The other had been a trail that simply dried up. Only the one reference to *magycke sylver* was ever made in Valentine Argentein's book, and Val had drawn a total blank on finding out anything else about him at all. It was as though he had existed only to produce one weedy little pamphlet and then vanished into thin air.

That and the improbably pertinent surname meant that the name Valentine Argentein was probably a pseudonym of some kind, but for whom? Nobody knew.

'No progress?' Val sniffed. 'Speak for yourself.'

I dropped the pen again. 'What? What did you find out?'

Val's chair drifted nearer. 'Nicolas Flamel,' she began.

'Argh,' I said.

'*Nicolas Flamel,*' Val repeated, 'May be of some use after all. Yes, I know he's credited with far more than he probably achieved, almost certainly did not create any "philosopher's stone", and is highly unlikely to have discovered an elixir of immortality.'

'I wish people would stop *obsessing* about him,' I grumped, sourly eyeing my book stack. You read about alchemy, you're going to read about Flamel. Every. Single. Time. And no one can even agree about whether or not he had any magick. He was most likely irrelevant to our entire investigation, but continued to obtrude, like a four-teenth-century French wall I couldn't see around.

'He is insufferably boring and cannot be defended for his omnipresence,' Val agreed, possibly with a shade of sarcasm. 'But, his *connections* are beginning to interest me. For example, did you know he was acquainted with Mary Werewode?'

'Mary Werewode— hang on—' I groped for my note-book, and flipped feverishly through its pages. I'd come across that name before, buried in an otherwise un-derwhelming book called *The Principles of Alchymistry.* 'Right. The lady laughing stock.' She'd been a low-ranking noblewoman in the late 1300s with an interest in natural philosophy. Society at the time wasn't so forgiving of women taking an interest in anything but home and hearth, so that might have been reason enough for her reputation. But what I'd read of her did sound pretty bizarre. For example, she believed that bathing naked under the full moon would restore her youth — something about absorbing *the gentle radiance* through her bare skin.

I can tell you, there's nothing in either science or magick that would allow for that. More's the pity.

Val, though, was grinning, a rather devilish expression. 'You should know, Ves. The shining lights of history were often considered cranks in their own time.'

'So Mary Werewode wasn't a crank?' I perked up. If there was the smallest possibility that a spot of naked moon-bathing would take a few years off *me*, I was up for it.

'I don't know yet,' Val cautioned. 'But Flamel is said to have corresponded with her, which means maybe she wasn't just spouting hot air. None of those letters seem to have survived, but there *is* one point of possible interest.' She set before me a slim volume, leather-bound and crusty with age. It had the delicate, feminine look of a ladies' journal.

'This is nowhere near old enough to be Mary Werewode's,' I said.

'It actually belonged to Cicily Werewode, who identifies herself as Mary's descendant. She appears to have been a great admirer of her great-great-grandmother's work, and expressed a strong desire to reproduce it.'

I eyed the book, sceptical. 'And Mary Werewode corresponded with Flamel. Are we talking more elixir-of-immortality nonsense?' Alchemists of the past seem to have come in two kinds, according to my reading. The kind that chased after elixirs and philosopher's stones — Flamel-style — and who possessed no actual magick with which to do it; and the kind we were more interested in, the witches and magicians of the past who had some magickal talent to bring to bear. It was the latter kind I'd been chasing, and failing to uncover. The lead-into-gold crowd had completely co-opted the term Alchemy, and even hundreds of years later that's all anyone talks about.

I suppose the big question is: was there any overlap between the two? I couldn't answer that one either.

'According to what she *says*,' insisted Val, perhaps noticing my slight abstraction. The heat, I tell you. It turns my brains to cotton-wool. 'Mary had no interest in the elixir of life, or any of that guff.'

'I find that hard to believe. She was known for trying to spin youth from moonlight.'

'Yes, but Cicily claims she deliberately spread these absurd notions about, in order to conceal what she was really doing.'

'You mean she *wanted* to be known as a crank?'

'The practice of alchemy didn't always make a person popular,' Val said. 'That might be one motive. And then, she may not have wanted to run the risk of someone else taking credit for her work.'

'You mean like somebody male.'

'It was a thing that happened.'

'Tell me about it.'

'Anyway, if Cicily is to be believed, nothing we've read about Mary Werewode had any basis in reality. *Cicily* was certainly a practitioner of magick, and she says Mary was, too. She claims her great-grandmother was a pioneer of magickal alchemy, preceding James Fryelond and Florian van der Linden by almost fifty years. And her speciality?' Val paused for effect.

'Yeeeees?' I said.

'*Silver,*' said Val. 'Which, according to Cicily, was another reason why Mary was laughed at. What kind of an alchemist wants to make silver when you could be making gold, or better yet diamonds?'

'The kind who knew about moonsilver!' I grabbed for the little book. Carefully. 'Hey, I wonder if her moon-bathing had some kernel of truth to it, too. Maybe she wasn't spreading absurd stories about herself. Maybe they were the truth, but they sounded so insane nobody believed them.'

'The word moonsilver seems to be specific to the Yllan-falen,' Val said, shaking her head. 'Cicily never uses it, and we have no reason to think Mary did either. So, probably not.'

'Damn.' Something about the very craziness of the idea appealed to me. 'Val, I swear you're a marvel. Where did you dig up this gem?' The two men she'd named, Fryelond and van der Linden, were legends in magickal alchemy (as far as that ever went) and as such had been our starting points. We'd both read their books from cover to cover, forwards and backwards, hoping to find something about magickal silver. But neither of them had even touched upon the subject, preferring only marginally successful attempts to turn pebbles into the kinds of imbued jewels Wands are made out of. We'd hit a wall. Again.

Had Val found a way forward?

'An obscure mention of an obscure mention,' said Val, shrugging. 'You know how that goes. I followed a trail through some journals and treatises, tracked down a sur-viving copy of this book in the catalogue of the Magickal Archives of the City of York, and requested a loan. It ar-rived this morning.'

And there you have it. Val is the best historical detective in the known world. 'Can I read it?' I asked, tenderly stroking the cover.

'You can, but I've already compiled notes about the salient parts. And I really think you should take a break.'

I looked sadly at the little book. I still wanted to read it, but Val was right. With cotton-wool for brains, I probably wouldn't achieve much by doing so.

'I take it the answers we want aren't in here,' I said. 'That would be far too easy.'

'No, that's the frustrating part. We know from Cicily that Mary Werewode devoted many years to the alchemical study of silver in some fashion, but Cicily is vague on the details.'

'Damn.'

'But.'

I held my breath. I love it when Val says something fabulously erudite, if disappointing, followed by a qualifying *but*. Some marvellous twist is always coming.

'This journal was written when she was a very young woman,' said Val. 'Scarcely twenty. She'd been investigating Mary's work for less than a year, and as yet I have no idea what became of her afterwards.'

'Ooooh.' My imagination raced away, picturing all the fabulous things Cicily Werewode might have gone on to do in the 1600s or whenever it was she'd lived. Perfected her ancestor's moon-bathing technique. Created reams upon reams of magickal silver, and helpfully left the recipe lying around somewhere for us to find. Discovered the elixir of immortality, and used it.

Regretfully, I discarded all my ideas. If she had done any such things, she would be a legend.

Unless... unless she, too, had kept her endeavours a secret.

Never mind. We had a trail to follow, and Library Detectives Val and Ves were on the case. I perked up. 'Why was it in York?' I said. 'Is that where the Werewodes lived?'

'Pertinent question, Ves,' said Val. 'I wondered that, too, and I'm looking into it.'

'I could look into it!' I beamed hopefully.

'You could, if you weren't just about to take a break.'

'But—'

'Go get some air, Ves. You look like a wrung-out dishcloth.'

'Ouch.'

'Harsh, but fair.' Val retrieved Cicily's journal, smoothly rotated her chair, and floated off back to her desk.

I hauled myself up from my chair, paused while my overheated head swam and my vision blurred, and finally stumbled my way towards the door. If I had to take a break, well then Jay was going to take a break with me.

2

'WHERE,' I SAID PLAINTIVELY, some twenty minutes later, 'is Jay?'

I'd searched most of the building for him, and then the gardens, too, and found no sign. Ending up at last in the first-floor common room, just in case I'd missed him before, I posed my question to the room at large.

Three people were there: Dave from the treasury (accounts, by any other name; Milady despises modern corporate-speak); lovely, Scary Rob; and a newcomer (she looked about five minutes old) that I didn't know.

Rob, parked by the open window with a tall glass of water at his elbow, looked up from the magazine he was reading. 'He's not here,' he said.

'I discovered that for myself just now.' I flopped into a chair, disconsolate. Searching the premises for Jay had only made me hotter, and without the satisfaction of sharing Val's breakthrough with him. 'So where is he?' I'd checked my phone, too, in case of missed messages from him, but there was nothing.

'He's off on assignment.'

I blinked. 'Without me?'

'He's with Melissa's team on some kind of artefact retrieval.'

'Oh,' I said.

Rob smiled, kindly enough, at my disappointment. 'He's the only Waymaster we have, Ves. You do realise how in demand he is? Every department at Home has been clamouring to borrow him for weeks.'

'Oh,' I said again.

'You were lucky to monopolise him for so long.'

I waved this away, duly humbled. 'Any idea when he'll be back?' I asked, super casually.

'Miss him?' said Rob.

'It's not that,' I said quickly.

'Mmhmm.' Rob went back to his magazine.

'It's just that we're starting to make a bit of a breakthrough on the alchemy thing, and we might need him soon.'

'Oh?' Rob looked up. 'Where are you going?'

'Possibly, York.'

'York isn't that far away.'

'You mean we should *drive* places? In a car? Old school.'

Rob grinned. 'You're getting spoiled.'

'I like my personal Waymaster service.'

'Uh huh. But you're in no way missing Jay.'

'I miss my *Waymaster*,' I sniffed. 'Who *happens* to be Jay.'

'Yes, and he isn't yours.'

What that meant, of course, was that Jay had graduated from the position of *new boy* and no longer particularly needed my guidance. He was a fully-fledged agent in his own right, and in great demand. Popular, too. I couldn't help noticing that everybody liked Jay.

'Lonesome?' said Rob.

'I am not lonely,' I said with imperious dignity.

He gave me much the same sceptical look I'd been getting from Val. He didn't say anything else, but he didn't need to. Val's essential point held. I'd spent months rattling about the world(s) with Jay, frequently Alban and Zareen, and more recently Emellana Rogan, too. Now Alban and Em were gone back to Mandridore, Zareen was in recovery at the School of Weird, and Jay was off saving the magickal world without me.

Maybe I was just the teensiest bit lonely.

At least I had Val. And Addie. I could feel my link with my unicorn pal, wrapped tenderly around my heart. She was my familiar, and I suppose I was hers; I always felt her near me, even when she probably wasn't. I'd taken more than one secret (hopefully) trip back to her glade to visit, and don my unicorn horn and tail myself. It felt good.

Possibly too good.

Rob was scrutinising me in that doctorly way of his. Looking for signs of ill-health, probably; Milady had given me stern instructions to rest. 'Do I need a check-up?' I asked him.

'I don't know,' he said easily. 'Are you feeling well?'

'Completely.' I flashed him my sunniest smile.

He was visibly unconvinced. 'Look,' he said, putting his magazine aside. 'If you want to talk to someone, I've given Grace notice to give you an appointment anytime. She'll see you whenever you want.'

'Grace?' I blurted. 'Why?'

He shrugged. 'Just in case.'

'Did Milady put you up to this?'

'She might have mentioned it.'

I said nothing more, fuming quietly. It wasn't that I had anything against Grace personally. It was just the fact that Grace Clement is our resident psychologist. When Rob spoke of an appointment, he meant an intake interview. Or in other words, Milady thought I might be losing my marbles.

I don't know quite why I felt offended by that, but I did.

Rob was waiting for an answer.

'I'll bear it in mind,' I said.

His dark eyes twinkled at me. 'You're annoyed.'

'Wouldn't you be?'

He thought about that for a moment. 'Only if I thought Milady might be right.'

'About what? That I'm a sandwich short of a picnic?'

'No, nothing like that. But, Ves, you've been through a lot lately. Things nobody knew were even possible. It would not be surprising if you were feeling a little... stressed.'

'I've had plenty of rest,' I said. 'I'm fine.'

Rob nodded. 'You should know that Jay saw her, before he left with Melissa.'

'Jay? What? Is he all right?'

'He's fine. He just needed a little help processing a few things.'

Small wonder. Jay had joined us only in April, and as luck would have it he'd arrived just in time to be dropped in at the deep end. *Way* at the deep end. He didn't have my ten-year experience of mad Society missions to help buffer the impact; he was fresh off the farm, so to speak. It was probably a good thing that he'd got some help.

I pushed aside some few, small, unworthy feelings — if Jay had been struggling, why hadn't he talked to *me*? — and focused on feeling glad that he was okay.

'Just think about it,' said Rob. 'Nobody's going to push you, so don't get mulish about it.'

'Mulish? Me? Never.' I stood up. 'You don't happen to know when Jay will be back, by any chance?'

'I don't think anyone does. He'll be back when they've finished whatever they're doing.'

I permitted myself a tiny sigh. 'Thanks, Rob.' I trailed off towards the door.

'Ves?' Rob said.

I stopped. 'Yes?'

'You can also just talk to me, if you feel more comfortable with that.'

I mulled that over. Maybe I would. I'd known Rob much longer than I'd known Grace, and we had been on several missions together. He had a solid, calm air about him that I found soothing, at least when he had his doctor hat on; not so much when he was in Scary Rob mode.

'I'll think about it,' I said. 'Thanks.'

I WENT UP TO my room. Someone had taped a page torn from a glossy mag onto my door.

Prince Alban Wows Europe, shouted the headline, and my heart quickened. He looked gorgeous, all princely splendour as he paid a state visit to some foreign troll kingdom or other.

He also had an unusual accessory. A woman almost as tall as he was stood at his side, decked in jewels and every inch a royal. Princess Marit, his wife.

My stomach dropped.

I snatched the page off my door and disappeared inside with it, retreating to my bed. I stared at the picture, hoping to find something to criticise. No luck. Marit was lovely, almost as beautiful as Alban was handsome, and with nothing of hauteur about her. Alban had implied that she was of a chilly disposition, but she didn't look it. She was smiling, a real smile, not a fake, gracious-princess grimace. They looked good together.

I wondered who had left the page for me.

'Right,' I told myself after about ten minutes of this. 'Get a grip, Ves.' I screwed up the page and threw it in the bin, then sauntered into the bathroom. Enough pining. I'd deal with my used-dishcloth status with a cool shower, head down to the cafeteria for lunch, then get back to the library. My break hadn't been quite the refreshing interlude Val had envisioned, and I'd about had enough of it.

FOUR HOURS LATER FOUND me back in the library and glued to a computer, Val had reserved to herself the task of combing through Cicily's journal again, looking for any clues she had missed. She also had three other books with her, the contents of which she would not tell me about. 'Not until I've had a look,' she'd insisted. 'I don't want to raise your hopes. Or mine.'

I didn't mind. My job was to scour the secret internet archives pertaining to magickal history, the kind that only Val had full access to. I'd been at it for hours already, and I had a long list of notes forming. None of them especially pertinent, but notes nonetheless. Notes are good.

'Any and all mentions of the Werewode family,' Val had said. 'Write them all down, Ves, especially any pertaining to the York area. Check family history records, too. I want to know if there were any other Werewodes of interest, and I *really* want to know what became of Cicily.'

'Probably marriage,' I'd suggested.

Hours later, I stuck by that surmise, with one modification: marriage or death. That's because I had found zero references to a Cicily Werewode after 1583, which was approximately when she had been writing her journal.

And when the women of history disappeared off the his-torical record like that, it usually meant they'd died — or undergone a marital name-change.

Unfortunately, marriage records don't really go back that far. We could consult the parish register for the area she had got married in, but for that we'd need to know where she came from. Sadly for my theory, that had not proved to be York.

Half an hour later, I had it. I didn't even have to dig through the magickal archives for this one; I found it in an obscure collection of birth and christening records from 1538 through to 1672. No marriage record for Cicily Werewode — but there was a birth. In the Yorkshire parish of Kirkby Malzeard, in 1590, a Godfrey Elvyng was born to Degare Elvyng and his wife, Cicily.

Elvyng. Middle name: Werewode.

I stared open-mouthed at the screen for fully a minute, barely breathing.

Then I rocketed out of my chair, and high-tailed it to Val's desk.

'Val,' I said. 'I've got it.'

She looked up, noted my expression of euphoric excite-ment, and sat straighter in her chair. 'Go on,' she said.

'Cicily Werewode was an Elvyng.'

'*What?*'

'She must've married Degare Elvyng — I couldn't find a marriage record for them but I found a birth record, there's a son—' I babbled on, probably making a confused mess of it but Val, to her credit, managed to follow me.

When I'd finished, she looked as electrified as I felt. 'And is this *the* Elvyng family?' she said.

'How many magickal families called Elvyng can there possibly be in Yorkshire?'

She nodded slowly, her face alight with an excitement echoing my own. 'Ves, you're amazing. This is huge. We *have* to be onto something.'

Onto something we were. See, York looms large among magickal communities of the modern age. It's been a centre of magick for centuries. It's home not only to the aforementioned Magickal Archives which Val has already been plundering, but also to the Elvyng Academy, an ancient school for certain magickal disciplines which *everybody* who's anybody has graduated from. And more. Lots more. There's an entire street called Elvyng Lane right in the heart of York, and it's a spot any magick user would kill to visit.

'Val,' I breathed. 'Tell me we're going shopping.'

'We are *not* going shopping.'

'Damnit.'

'We are going on a serious, scholarly field trip.'

'Yes.' I adopted a suitably serious expression.

'And if we should happen to pass by the most famous magick shop in Britain on the way, we cannot be held responsible for the consequences.'

'Now you're talking.'

3

'Ves,' snapped Val the following morning, ten o'clock sharp, somewhere in the midst of the city of York. 'Calm down. They aren't going to be there.'

'They might be,' I protested. 'Well, maybe not all of them. One of them? It could happen.'

'The Elvyngs have more important things to do than hover about in The Shambles signing autographs.'

'Hovering,' I beamed. 'Literally.'

'No.'

'I don't want an autograph. I just want to…' I paused. 'I don't even know.'

'Gush about how amazing they are, knowing you.'

'You think me absurd. I knew it.'

'Ves, everyone thinks you're absurd.'

'Except Alban. *He* thinks I'm impressive.' I wanted to add Jay's name to the (incredibly short) list; he'd shown signs of looking up to me when he'd first arrived. But I had pretty much put paid to that by now. Nobody who's seen me and a plate of cake in the same room together could hold me in respect for long.

'He does,' said Val, widening her eyes at me. 'That's a thought. Think your Baron could get us an introduction to Crystobel Elvyng?'

'He isn't my Baron, and no.'

'No?'

'He isn't here.'

'Where is he?'

'Touring Europe with his wife.'

'Ah.' Val, wisely, let the subject drop. 'No matter. If we need to talk to the Elvyngs, Milady will arrange it.'

The car drew to a stop in a side street, and our driver came round to let us out. Val used a proper wheelchair outside the grounds of Home, and we spent the first few minutes of our sojourn in York getting her set up in it. I'd witch it as soon as we got out of the regular city, so she wouldn't have to roll the thing around.

'Right,' I said as our driver — her name was Candice — departed again with the car. I took hold of the handles of Val's chair, ready to wheel. My fingers fizzed, and the chair jumped a foot in the air and began to levitate.

'Ves,' hissed Val. 'Not yet.'

'Sorry, I didn't mean to—' I spoke softly to the chair and it settled down, permitting me to wheel it like a normal person once more.

This has been happening lately. Ever since I'd soaked up all that excess magick on the Fifth, in fact (almost blowing myself up in the process). A surge of something jazzy happens; there's a fizz of magick; and anything I touch is in for an interesting time.

I made a mental note to spend an afternoon at Addie's glade somewhere over the weekend.

'Which way?' I said, grasping the wheelchair's handles firmly. My fingers had stopped fizzing. Probably it would be fine.

'Why are you asking me?' she said.

'Because you know everything.'

The shameful truth was, I'd only been to Elvyng Lane once before, about a year after my induction into the Society. It wasn't lack of interest that had prevented my ever making a return visit. It was lack of everything else. Impulse control, willpower, funds...

Val consulted her phone, then pointed. 'That way, and turn left.'

We made slow progress in this fashion, pausing from time to time to check our bearings. The streets of York were busy, surprisingly so for the early morning. Summer holidays, of course. At length we made it to The Shambles, which is a crooked little street dating back something like a thousand years. Timber-framed buildings overhang the street, some of them pretty old — as in fourteenth century, Mary Werewode's era.

Val and I quietly slipped between a chocolate shop and a tiny gallery, and, as far as the other shoppers were concerned, disappeared.

Don't ask me how. I'm sorry, but it is a deep, dark secret and I'm not allowed to share.

Elvyng Lane is a bit of a misnomer by now. Maybe it was just an alley, once, but these days it's more of a courtyard. We emerged from the secret snickelway into an airy square, lined on all four sides with buildings. The most imposing of them is the Elvyng Academy, a three-storey pile built in Elizabethan red brick with those wonderful twisty chimney-pots. It was founded (according to my hurried swatting on the way) in 1557 by Wauter Elvyng, father of Degare. Cicily's father-in-law.

Ranged around the rest of the courtyard were such delights as the Magickal Archives of the City of York (whither we were bound), Gryffen's bookshop (legendary for grimoires), and of course the Elvyng Emporium. The place that almost bankrupted me about nine years ago.

I resolutely turned my face away from the latter's inviting façade and marched off in the direction of the Archives.

'Ves,' hissed Val when we were halfway across the square. 'They've got new chairs.'

'Don't tempt me,' I begged, 'or we may never get out of here alive. I'll just move in and stay there forever and ever until I die of thirst. Or maybe longing.'

'Chairs,' said Val again, and gasped. 'Green brocade — Ves, that chair is waving at me. Stop. Stop!'

I gritted my teeth. 'What was it you said about serious scholarly field trip?'

'*Very* serious,' said Val. 'Right after we get me a new chair.'

'No. Work first, shopping later.'

'Who are you and what have you done with Ves?'

'This is the new Ves. The old one was absurd, remember?'

We were by this time safely across the square, the mesmerising Emporium behind us. Once we had passed through the grand doors of the Archives, and were out of sight of the magick shop, I judged it safe to charm Val's chair. It rose a couple of inches, hovering nicely.

Val needed a couple of minutes to recover her dignity. I didn't interrupt.

At length she gave a tiny sigh, and said: 'Do you think it's possible I spend too much time in libraries?'

'No.'

'Do you think it's possible *you* spend too much time in libraries?'

'I—' I stopped. I wanted to say no again, but hadn't I been complaining about exactly that only just yesterday? 'We're here for a good reason,' I said instead, chickening out.

'I finally get out of the House,' grumbled Val, floating off towards the reception desk. 'And the first thing I do is disappear into the Archives.'

This was unlike Val, so I ignored it. She was just grouchy about the chair. And maybe some other things too, for all I knew. She floated up to the desk — and stopped three feet short, before abruptly turning around again and making for the door.

'Val!' I took off after her, reaching her only as she sailed out into the street. 'Forget the chair! You already have a *great* one.'

'No,' said Val. 'This is not where we need to be.' She paused on the doorstep, her eyes scanning the square. To my relief, she did not seem inordinately interested in the Emporium this time.

'Er,' I said. 'If we want information, the Archives are *always* a good port of call. Surely?'

'Not this time. Think about it, Ves. We aren't here just to poke into the history of the Elvyngs, interesting as it no doubt is. We're here about Cicily Werewode-Elvyng's work, specifically anything derived from Mary Werewode. And, of course, anything the Elvyng descendants might have accomplished since. I already asked the archivists for anything else with the Werewode name, and they have nothing. The other thing they do not have is an Elvyng archive. I know this, because it's frustrated me before. That family is secretive.'

'There might be books from after her marriage in there—' I began.

'No. If the Elvyngs had developed a way to make magickal silver and they were interested in bragging about the fact, we'd already know. Everyone would know. They're *famous*, and moonsilver is exactly the kind of expensive rarity they'd sell in the Emporium if they were minded to profit from it. If they have any materials on this subject at all, they've been sitting on them for generations. They aren't going to be lying around on a shelf in the public archives.'

'All right,' I allowed. 'That makes sense. But then, why did we come?'

'To do some digging, right at the heart of the Elvyng empire. For once, Ves, we must be strong, and ignore the big, beautiful library.'

'It's okay,' I said. 'I like digging.'

'So. If you were a scion of a famous magickal family with limitless resources at your disposal, where would *you* put a library of secret alchemical research?'

'Why would I bother having it at all if I wasn't going to use it?'

'Good point. Then they're using it — somehow.'

'Or, it doesn't exist.'

Val shook her head. 'Cicily was a dedicated scholar, and alchemy was her subject. Mary Werewode favoured silver as her focus, Cicily did too, and I can't believe she would have abandoned her work.'

'After marriage? She wouldn't have been the first woman to do so.'

'True,' sighed Val.

'Especially likely,' I added, after a moment's thought, 'if she was championing the work of a woman history remembered as a crank. Would her husband and father-in-law have taken it seriously, either? If not: would that have stopped her, or might she have gone on in secret?'

'She might have,' said Val slowly. 'Either because the work was considered risible, or — because it was not. Look at that place.' She waved a hand at the glorious Emporium, inviting as it was, and dripping with money and magick. 'All this wealth and grandeur had to come from somewhere, and the Emporium's four hundred years old. They had an eye for valuables, to say the least.'

'And a talent for profiting from them,' I agreed. 'Could she have feared that they'd do the same with her own and Mary's work?'

'Who knows. But altogether, I think it plausible that Cicily Werewode might have had a cache of secret research somewhere, which the Elvyngs may or may not know about.'

'I wonder,' I said slowly, going off on a minor mental tangent, 'if they have any magickal silver artefacts in stock today?'

Val sucked in a breath. 'Surely not. Do you *know* how rare such things are nowadays?'

'Yes, but only as of recently. I don't really know where I'm going with this, but... magickal silver seems to be a lost idea in general, no? Not only do we have no idea how to make it — if there was ever a way — but the magickal world in general has forgotten that it exists. Including the Elvyngs?'

'If they knew about it *and* knew how to make it, we'd all know,' Val agreed, and nodded towards the Emporium. 'Look at that place. The windows would be full of the stuff.'

'So either, Cicily's work never bore fruit and we're chasing a red herring. Or, whatever she achieved was lost somewhere in the past five hundred years.'

'Pessimistic, Ves,' chided Val. 'We've got Cicily's journal. She must have produced other documents over her lifetime. Where would they have gone?'

'They would have been absorbed into the Elvyng papers, most likely,' I said. 'Which, if they're not in the Archives, must be...'

'In one of the other Elvyng buildings,' said Val. 'Of which there are several.'

'And!' I said, not entirely listening. 'Val, how did Cicily know about Mary Werewode's work in the first place? She must have had something of Mary's, too, something that indicated what she was doing. And if those things aren't in the Archives, then—'

'Then *those* might be with the Elvyng papers, too,' said Val, sitting upright. 'Yes! These ancient old families have boxes and boxes of such records lying about, and nobody ever cares to go through them. Anything important would be locked away, but crumbling notes on improbable subjects written by women nobody remembers or respects?'

'What we want could be lying in an attic somewhere, just waiting to be found.'

'So back to my earlier question,' said Val.

'If I was impossibly rich and spectacularly magickal, where would I store my junk?'

'Exactly.'

'I wasn't actually joking about the attic.'

As one, we turned to look at the Elvyng Academy.

'It's said to have been founded in Wauter Elvyng's own house,' I said. 'They had only four students to begin with, and they weren't that rich yet. They didn't have the means to buy a whole new property for it.'

'Cicily might have lived there,' said Val.

'Almost certainly did,' I agreed.

'Do you think it's too late to be admitted as students?'

'Yes.' I said this with some regret. As a child I'd dreamed of attending the Elvyng Academy — we all did — but the entry requirements would make your eyes bleed to look at them. I hadn't been up to it. 'We can, however, wave the Society flag and hope they find us impressive,' I added.

'If you can impress the Prince of Mandridore, you can impress the Elvyngs.'

'Or their head teacher, anyway. Got your Important Person face on?'

Val drew herself up in her chair. I don't know about me, but *she* can be imposing as hell when she wants to be. 'Let's go.'

4

To my surprise, when we entered the illustrious Academy building we found the entrance hall full of people. And I do mean full. They weren't students either, or they didn't look like it. Most were at least my age or older, and only about half were human. The rest were fae of various tribes and cultures, including a couple of spriggans, a troll, and a willowy silver-haired man who would've looked right at home in the kingdoms of the Yllanfalen. I'd expect to see such a rabble pouring through the doors of the Emporium, but what were they doing here at the Academy?

A petite woman with a blonde ponytail and a thousand-watt smile spotted us as we came in, and leapt to clear room for Val's chair. 'Are you here for the tour?' she asked us.

'N—' began Val.

'*Yes,*' I said firmly. 'We'd love to join the tour.' Not only were tours sometimes surprisingly informative, but the general chaos they caused was also perfect for surreptitiously sneaking off. Nobody would notice if a tour of twenty-plus people suddenly shrank by, say, one or two.

'Great!' said the tour guide, displaying enough energy for twelve people as she herded us all into a roughly organised group, and took up a position at the front. She placed Val front and centre, which was both considerate and convenient. We got a clear view of everything, even in the crowd.

The Academy building was not quite what I had pictured. It *was* small, relatively speaking, and I had no trouble believing that it had once been a private residence. The walls were built from that lovely, dark-red brick they favoured in the 1500s, at least those who could afford it; those things were painstakingly crafted by hand, after all. The leaded windows looked original, and the place had the eccentric, poky structure of antiquity; none of the clear, open spaces and featureless décor one would expect to find in a modern educational establishment. The Elvyngs hadn't stinted on ornaments, either. Oil paintings hung in ornate frames upon every wall, probably depicting former scions of their line, and I spotted more than one artefact of great age and value prominently upon display.

They must have good security at the Elvyng Academy — and a charming confidence in the rectitude of their students.

Hopefully the security wasn't going to get in my way later. I had nothing like so much faith in my own rectitude. Oh, not that I was planning to walk off with a fourteenth-century enchanted music box (tempted though I might be). But a little sneaking and stealthing might well be in order.

'Welcome to the Elvyng Academy!' roared our tour guide, and the low babble of chatter and rustling of fidgeting people slowly ceased. 'Over the next half-hour I'll be showing you the highlights of this remarkable, early sixteenth-century building, home to generations of the brightest minds in magick. The Elvyng family's contributions to magick are deservedly legendary, and you'll be hearing all about those today.

'It *is* the summer holidays so most classes are suspended this week. There *may* be one or two study groups still in session, so I must ask you *please* to keep the chatter to a minimum as we proceed. Okay?' Tour Guide Lady beamed upon us.

We were an obedient tour group, for nobody spoke.

'Okay, let's begin!' Tour Guide Lady led us out of the main hall and into a kind of salon, its contents correct for the sixteenth century: heavy, English oak chests and cabinet chairs, tapestries, etc. More paintings, the largest of which we halted in front of.

'The Elvyng family legacy began with Ambrose Elvyng in the late fourteen hundreds,' said Tour Guide Lady. I caught a glimpse of her nametag. Denise. 'An early pioneer of the arts of charm-binding, he's said to have been among the first to lastingly imbue inanimate objects with magickal properties. Isn't that impressive? But it was his son, Wauter Elvyng, and his daughter Godlefe who founded the Elvyng Academy...'

Blah blah blah. I stopped listening, having already read much of this information off the internet. Keeping half an ear open for any mention of Cicily or the Werewodes, I devoted myself to a surreptitious study of the contents of an impromptu bookcase set up atop a heavy oak chest behind Denise. Between two weighty bookends of imbued crystal were half a dozen reasonably aged-looking books.

Great Expectations, Gulliver's Travels, Jane Eyre...
Novels.

I suppose it was too much to hope that a book titled *Magickal Silver and How to Make it* would be lying there waiting for me, but was an interesting magickal tome or two just *too* much to ask of the Elvyngs?

Feeling obscurely piqued, I folded my arms.

'What about Cicily Werewode?' Val said, firmly interrupting Denise as she streamed smoothly onto the next topic. 'She married Degare Elvyng, didn't she?'

'I believe so,' beamed Denise.

'What can you tell us about connections between the Elvyng family and the Werewodes?' said Val.

Denise's smile faltered. 'Uh, there are no *known* connections with a family of that name, but I believe there *is* a portrait of Cicily Elvyng in the house. Perhaps in one of the bedchambers?'

'We would like to see that,' declared Val.

Denise's smile returned. 'I'm afraid that won't be included as part of this tour. Now! If you'll follow me into the conservatory...'

Val shot me a meaningful look. Probably it said, *so much for your bright idea of joining the tour.*

'Sorry,' I mouthed.

Val shook her head, rolled her eyes, and made an awkward jerking motion in the direction of the upstairs. Then she sailed after the vanishing crowd of tourists.

Oh. Right.

Val couldn't hope to sneak away without her absence being noted; not after she'd been given so prominent a position at the front of the tour, and being the only person in a wheelchair at that. But *I* could.

Portrait of Cicily Werewode. Right.

I waited until the rest of my tour group had disappeared through the far door after Denise, then quietly retreated back the way we'd come in. I'd glimpsed a set of stairs leading off one of the passageways we had passed through, which to my relief proved easy to find again (this is me we're talking about, here. If anyone could get lost in the space of two rooms and a couple of passageways it would be me). I stole up to the first floor, blessing my random choice to wear flat, sneaking sandals instead of the heels I'd briefly considered. Thanks to the summer holidays, I encountered no one as I wandered into room after room.

I soon concluded I was still on the wrong floor. If any of these chambers had been bedrooms once, they were classrooms now, and none of them featured portraits on the walls. It took me ten minutes to find more staircases up, and I began to feel a little nervous of the time. How long would the tour take? Would anybody notice I was no longer in the group? Val could cover for me, but still... I darted up more stairs, and found myself at last on a floor with a certain air of neglect about it. Dustier than the floors below, and much less decorated, it looked little used and little valued; the deep blue carpets covering the floors were faded and threadbare, and nothing had benefited from a coat of paint in a while.

It was also much more cramped. I was entering the roof space, I judged, for the ceilings were lower and sloping.

Servants were probably housed here, once, and now? Storage space. The kind of place boxes of old papers might be kept. And old, forgotten bedchambers nobody now had a use for.

I opened a door at random — and stopped, arrested. I'd found a bedchamber, but so small it bordered upon classifiable as a garret. The furniture, simple and inexpensive, included a narrow bed with faded green tapestry curtains, a lone oak chest, and a couple of blue plastic chairs incongruously dumped in a corner.

A portrait hung by the window. Circular, mean in proportion and poorly maintained, the image was darkened with age and dirt; however, the subject matter shone through to my interested eye. It showed a woman's face in profile, her pale hair crimped and braided according to the fashions of the fifteen hundreds. The portrait itself excited no especial remark, being a merely workmanlike piece of art; but the subject matter had me across the room in seconds, examining it more closely with breathless interest.

The woman was not human.

Or, not *only* human. The shape of her face was human enough, and though only her head, neck and shoulders were depicted, nothing suggested she was of other than ordinary human stature. But that hair was unusual: still pale blonde, despite the layers of grime coating the image. Were it cleaned, the woman's hair would likely prove to be silvery in hue. Her eyes, too, could pass for blue, but were shaded with amethyst. I couldn't have said what else it was about her that gave her ancestry away; something about her bone structure, perhaps, or even just some species of intuition with which we're all occasionally blessed. But like the willowy man I'd seen below, the woman in the painting would not have looked too out of place among the Yllanfalen.

The Elvyngs had an Yllanfalen ancestress.

And somehow, I knew in my heart that this was Cicily Werewode. The era was right, the clothes she wore, everything.

'Cicily,' I breathed, lightly touching the carved oak frame. What was she doing, exiled all the way up here? Why was her husband so celebrated, and not she? Doubt washed over me. Were we right to think that Cicily Werewode had been onto something with her ancestress's work? Or that she had continued to pursue it even after marriage? Perhaps she wasn't, or hadn't. Perhaps she had got married and given everything else up, as so many women had chosen to — or been obliged to.

But her obvious Yllanfalen ancestry suggested otherwise. I paused, thoughts awhirl, as disparate pieces of this puzzle swirled around my mind.

The Yllanfalen. At least one of their kingdoms — my mother's, at present — had a magickal silver artefact that was of paramount importance to their culture. The lyre was so old, nobody really knew where it had come from, save that a mythical king out of legend was said to have created it. Well; had he used mined magickal silver, or had he — or someone of his court — created the silver, too? The possibility hadn't crossed my mind before. But in my (admittedly not exhaustive) experience, the Yllanfalen were the only people who seemed to remember the Silver at all.

Mary Werewode. If Cicily had Yllanfal blood, had Mary also? How closely linked were the Werewodes to the Yllanfalen?

Mary and her moon-bathing. Moonsilver.

Skysilver? What had Mum actually called the stuff?

Both, I realised. She'd spoken of both. The *lyre* she talked of as made from "moonsilver", and the syrinx pipes — like my own — were "skysilver". I hadn't asked what those things were, at the time, nor what the difference between them was supposed to be. But perhaps there was no difference. The names were a matter of legend only, they sounded good in a story — but in essence they were both the substance we were now calling (rather drearily, in contrast) magickal silver.

Hmm.

Had Mary Werewode favoured silver because she was Yllanfalen? That would explain why she had gone in so different a direction to every other alchemist of her era, eschewing mere gold in favour of a "Silver" far more valuable, to those who realised it. But most didn't, hence the lack of respect in which she and her work were held.

Cicily had realised it. Had her husband? Had any of the Elvyngs? I'd never heard that the Elvyng family had any Yllanfalen connections. The influence of Cicily's other heritage had long since disappeared.

I chewed a fingernail, my eyes still fixed to the strange, pale face of Cicily Werewode. Had the sixteenth-century Elvyngs had any idea what Cicily was talking about, or not? Had any of them taken her work seriously? Had she been permitted to pursue it at all? If so, where were the results of it now?

These were questions that urgently needed answering.

Then again, maybe it didn't matter. Maybe alchemy alone wasn't the answer. Maybe we needed to go looking for the Silver among the Yllanfalen.

Moved by some strange (and reprehensible) impulse, I stretched out my hand once more, and let my fingertips lightly rest upon the surface of the canvas. One does not, ordinarily, go about feeling up delicate articles of great age; even the slightest interference can damage them. I cannot say why I so violated all such principles this time; only that I felt an odd desire to link myself with the enigmatic figure of Cicily Werewode, even if only for a moment.

And what a moment for my fingers to fizz.

Fffupht. Magick spurted. I snatched my hand away, but too late: a ripple of eerie light flooded Cicily's face, momentarily obscuring her features. When it faded, it left traces behind: a faint glimmer here and there, like motes of moonlight woven in her pale hair.

The dirt of centuries was gone. Cicily's face smiled at me, clear and vivid, fresh as the day her image was captured in paints.

I waited, breathless with anticipation. But the seconds ticked by and nothing else happened, save that the light faded from Cicily Werewode's hair.

I turned away at last, reluctant to leave so alluring, so vibrant a woman alone in this dingy little garret.

5

DEAR MUM, RAN MY text. *Can we please borrow a couple of your best alchemists. URGENT.*

'Think she will answer?' said Val.

'There's almost no chance of it.'

Val had been waiting in the Academy's entrance hall when I had finally made it downstairs, the tour having ended several minutes before. Denise must have noticed my absence *then*, if not sooner, but Val did not seem perturbed. She sat serenely near the door, unruffled. Only I knew her well enough to detect the signs of extreme boredom.

'Riveting tour, then?' I murmured as I hurried to join her.

Val gave me a sour look. 'I hope you appreciate the sacrifice I've made for you.'

'For *us*, Val. For the cause! Wait 'til you hear what I found.' I grabbed her chair and whooshed us out the door, waving cheerily to the woman on reception as we passed. Fortunately, there was no sign of Denise.

'It had better be good,' Val said once we were back outside in the sun. 'I had to hear every sodding detail of Crystobel Elvyng's life.'

'Academic career?'

'If she isn't the single most brilliant woman in magick, it isn't for lack of trying.'

'Childhood exploits?'

'Avid tree-climber, isn't that adorable?'

'Favourite brand of underwear?'

'Calvin Klein.'

I stopped. 'Really?'

'No.'

'Small mercies. Anyway, here's the scoop. I found *zero* promising-looking boxes of papers dumped at the back of a forgotten garret, *but*—' I ran quickly down my discovery and my list of not-quite-conclusions, or *nearly baseless speculations* by any other name. When I said them all out loud, they suddenly sounded ridiculous.

But Val nodded along, her head bobbing with each of my major points as we trundled around the square. When I'd finished, she said (to my secret relief): 'You really might be onto something there, Ves.'

I punched the air.

'Milady requisitioned some alchemist from the Court at Mandridore, no?' she continued.

'Yes, and maybe she ought to purloin a few from some other Court, too. Like Mum's.'

'Just what I was thinking.'

So I sent the text, just in case Mum was paying attention. And since she almost certainly wouldn't be, I also sent a note to Rob. It read: *Ves & Val reporting. Strongly advise Milady requests a prominent Yllanfalen alchemist to attend at Home.*

On second thought I added: *If there are any.* After all, I'd never heard of anyone bothering with alchemy in recent memory; but Milady had claimed the contrary. No one *publicly* bothered with it anymore, but that said nothing about private endeavour.

I wondered whether secret alchemical endeavour had played a part in the Society's recent history, and why no one had told me about it if it had. Van der Linden had never fully succeeded at turning worthless rubbish into priceless magickal jewels, and had eventually abandoned the project; his having done so was generally credited as the turning of the tide, the point where the magickal community turned away from alchemy, and began to see it as foolish.

But what if some part of his work had borne some kind of fruit after all, and was even now being employed across Britain? Or even just at Home?

Cursed secrets. I mean, I do get why alchemy's such an enthralling idea. Who wouldn't love to turn ordinary pebbles into ethereal rubies? Or lead into gold?

A reply came. Rob.

Why am I playing messenger boy?

Because Jay isn't Home.

Nothing else after that. I hoped he would pass the message along, but if not, I could do that myself soon enough.

First, though: the Emporium.

What, you thought Val and I would pass up the chance to break our hearts over the Elvyngs' unaffordable luxury goods?

Val might manage to be that sensible, but I certainly couldn't.

'About my chair,' said Val, veering in the direction of the Emporium's glittering doors.

All right, maybe not.

I made one last, feeble attempt to assert my inner sense of self-preservation. 'Val, you know we can't afford anything in there.'

'Speak for yourself,' said Val, and then she was through the doors, and what could a poor, weak Ves do but follow?

'Hi,' said Jay, and smiled.

'Argh,' I replied, jumping back about a foot.

'Did I startle you? Sorry.' He stood just inside the shining doors, hands in the pockets of his ever-present leather jacket, which was a wise move. Safely pocketed hands cannot reach longingly for impossible things.

'I thought you were...' I racked my brains. 'Somewhere else?'

'Wales. We pulled a charmed seventeenth-century chalice out of a crumbly local museum. They had it stuffed at the back of an exhibit called *Women at home in the fifteen hundreds.*'

My lips twitched. 'Did you have any trouble liberating it?'

'Not once they heard what we were offering.'

'Show me a museum that isn't strapped for cash and I'll show you...' I paused, struggling to think of something more improbable than that.

Jay grinned. 'Flying pigs?'

'I could actually show you flying pigs.'

'I don't think the pigs would like it.'

'Might depend on the pig. Anyway, what are you doing in York?'

'Waiting for you. I got back this morning, and Rob said you were headed for Elvyng Lane.'

'Uh huh. How did you know we'd come in here?'

Jay just looked at me.

'In my defence, it's Val who lost her head over a levitating green brocade chair.' I looked around, but couldn't see her around the milling shoppers. That, and my eye snagged on a glittering grimoire crusted with jewels, and everything else went out of my head.

'Do you need a security escort?' said Jay.

'Urgently.'

Jay saluted. 'What are we shopping for?'

'Whatever my greedy little heart desires.'

'So in other words, everything.'

'Just about.'

I EMERGED WITH NOTHING in hand, and about five hundred new additions to my wish list.

'I'm sort of proud of you,' said Jay as we hightailed it back to the relative safety of the square.

'For not buying anything?'

'Looks like self-restraint to me.'

'Are you implying I'm bad at that?'

Jay coughed. 'Er, not at all.'

Jay hadn't made any purchases either, though he had been as enchanted by a bespelled book box as I had been by my bejewelled grimoire. I couldn't blame him. The box's charms not only proposed to keep the contents preserved against the deleterious effects of time, but would actual-ly restore them to freshly-printed perfection, albeit very slowly. Imagine that. Ten years or so in Jay's box and even the crumbliest tome might be brand new again. Or at least, less decrepit.

The price tag was about half my yearly salary.

Sorrowfully, we left it untouched.

'That box reminds me a bit of what Fenella was talking about,' I mused, not at all reluctant to change the subject away from my personal weaknesses.

'You mean her restoration magick? Right. Though the box does it in a small way and at a snail's pace.'

Out on the Fifth, Fenella had achieved a similar effect upon an entire room, and quickly too. I sighed a little, wistful once more for the potency of magick in that far-off Britain.

'Have we lost Val?' said Jay, turning cautiously towards the Emporium again.

I risked a glance. No Val.

'Possibly for all of time,' I said. Then a glimpse of a familiar spring-green colour caught my eye, and there came Val, sailing out of the shop in the arms of the brocade chair she'd fallen in love with a few hours before.

I swear, I've never seen so smug a smile before in my life.

'Mortgaged house and home?' I said as she drifted up. I wasn't even joking, either. Up close, the chair's craftsmanship was exquisite, the fabric was expensive with a capital E, and a glance was enough to tell me that its levitation charms far outstripped my own, not inconsiderable efforts. She glided up, smooth as silk, and I imagined the word "comfortable" didn't even begin to cover it.

'I may have to sleep on the street,' Val said. 'But it was worth it, Ves. It was worth it.'

I had no trouble believing that.

BACK AT HOME, WE hit the library again, hard. Val wanted to scour the catalogues — yet again — for anything about the Werewodes or, indeed, the Elvyngs. I wanted to research the kingdoms of the Yllanfalen, and any historical proclivity for alchemical pursuits that I fervently hoped to uncover.

We both came up empty. Val found nothing but the usual info about the illustrious magickal family: much the same spiel that we'd been given on the tour. They certainly had their public image down pat.

I found far too *much* about the Yllanfalen, little of which looked relevant, but who could tell? It might take weeks to dig up and read every word of every available resource, and with no guarantee of coming up with any answers.

So I went back to badgering my mother. Seeing as she hadn't replied to my previous message, I attacked her again.

What's the use of being a faerie princess if I can't cadge favours off Her Majesty, my Mum?

I set my phone on the edge of my desk, and went back to my book. The Yllanfalen were secretive and reclusive, I discovered (you don't say), and while their kingdoms had been relatively welcoming in some halcyon past, the modern kingdoms rarely granted access to outsiders (perfect for my mother, then). They excelled at music-based enchantments and charms—

My phone buzzed.

Cordelia, Mum had written. *You are not a faerie princess. Remember? You refused.*

I know, I returned. *I just wanted to annoy you so you'd talk to me.*

Mum: *What do you want with alchemists?*

Me: *Something nefarious and deeply disturbing.*

Mum: *We don't have any.*

Me: *Okay, something heroic and spectacular.*

Mum: *Ves. Why the hell would I have an alchemist at court?*

Me: *You really don't have any?*

Mum: *I. Don't. Have. An. Alchemist.*

Damn.

Mum: *Nobody's done alchemy since about 1781.*

Me: *Fine, get me an Yllanfalen alchemist from 1781.*

Mum: *You do know that the elixir of immortality was a crock of shit?*

Me: *You are no help whatsoever.*

Mum: *Maybe I would be if I knew what this was about.*

Me: *We want to make magickal silver.*

Mum: *What?*

Me: *Magickal silver. You know, moonsilver. Or skysilver, whichever.*

Mum: *Make it? You can't make it. That's absurd.*

Me: *Why is it absurd?*

But that, apparently, was it. I'd exasperated my mother beyond enduring, and she'd thrown her phone down the toilet in disgust.

If I wanted an Yllanfalen perspective on alchemy, I'd have to look beyond my mother's kingdom.

On a hunch, I turned to a map of Yllanfalen territory from 1562, or a facsimile thereof. Val wouldn't let me have the original, for some reason. I'm sure it had nothing whatsoever to do with my habit of eating sweets at my desk.

The Yllanfalen had several kingdoms back in the day, and—

'Ves.' Jay had come in; I hadn't noticed.

'Huusshh,' I whispered. 'I'm on the brink of an exciting breakthrough.'

'You mean like this one?' Jay put a piece of paper down in front of me, half covering my map.

I flicked it aside, pointing. 'If the Werewodes were part Yllanfalen, that suggests there was probably one of their kingdoms in the Yorkshire area in the medieval era. Right? And look, there's one not all that far from York itself, at least in 1562—'

'Aylligranir,' said Jay.

I looked up, blinking. 'Right. How did you—?'

'Apparently our ideas were running along similar lines.' He tapped the page he'd given me, which I had disgracefully dismissed.

At the top was written *Aylligranir* in Jay's neat handwriting. It was underlined. Below it followed a list of facts: *Mentioned 1442 by Amhar Edris*, and similar entries; and at the end of the list, *Current monarch: Llirriallon the Gentle.*

Being Jay, he had also noted the locations of a known entrance, together with directions from the nearest henge.

'Star pupil,' I said, beaming.

'I'm not really a p— never mind. Ready to go?'

'Uh. Now?'

'If we don't go now, we don't go at all. It's only a matter of time before I'm dispatched to Land's End, or possibly Timbuktu.'

'What does Milady say?'

'She hasn't found an Yllanfalen alchemist yet.'

'In that case,' I said, rising from my chair. 'Let's swoop in and save the day.'

6

Ayliigranir. Courtesy of Jay, we whooshed up into West Yorkshire in no time, and courtesy of Addie we arrived at the historic entrance to the ancient kingdom of Aylligranir within about an hour.

So far, so good.

Next problem.

'How do we get in?' I said, gazing hopelessly at the sheer hillside before us. We were deep in the Yorkshire Dales, and all those people who claim that Yorkshire is the most beautiful county in England are really onto something. The sky positively glittered with sunshine; the grassy slopes were the vivid green of summer dreams; and the air smelled of... I don't know, heaven.

I wasn't an unhappy woman in that moment, except for the fact that I had no idea what to do next. For the hills, while beautiful, were also impenetrable, and though I strained every magickal sense I possessed, no sign of a way forward could I detect.

Reclusive, huh? I'm not sure that quite covers it.

'I've... no idea,' said Jay, dashing my hopes. When even the navigator is stumped, what does one do?

I sat down in the grass, cross-legged, and unwrapped one of the sandwiches we'd brought with us. Maybe I thought the comforting flavours of egg mayonnaise and cress might help me think.

'Oh, we're eating?' Jay stood regarding me in some exasperation, though he was not absolutely devoid of a smile.

It occurred to me that he looked tired. Nothing serious; just a slight droop in posture, an extra shadow or two about the eyes. But while I had been firmly ensconced in the library for weeks in order to "get some rest", albeit the scholarly kind, Jay had been working as usual. As our sole Waymaster, was that always going to be the case?

I patted the grass beside me. 'If you can't beat them, join them,' I said, offering him a sandwich.

He took it, and sat holding it, and staring at the hillside. The verdant slope was criss-crossed with those unfathomable drystone walls, the kind that consist of stones piled atop one another and which by some mysterious force do not fall down again. There were sheep, woolly and dozing in the sun. Lovely.

'Sandwiches taste a lot better if you put them in your mouth,' I suggested.

Jay ignored that. 'Did you find anything in all those books you were drowning in?'

'No. Lots about how much they don't like visitors, though.'

'The lack of signposts was a bit of a clue there.'

'Ring the bell for Aylligranir,' I intoned, picturing a sign bearing this very legend in glowing magickal lettering.

Jay took a bite of egg mayo.

'Then again,' I said, a stray wisp of thought stirring somewhere within. 'A bell. Maybe I'm onto something. They *are* primarily known for musical magicks.'

'I see no bell,' Jay observed.

'Me neither, but for a community of hermits that would be far too obvious.' I packed away my sandwich wrapping, and leapt to my feet.

'That was energetic,' said Jay, notably not following my example.

'I am on fire with possibility,' I informed him, retrieving my syrinx pipes from the bodice of my dress. I hadn't thought to bring my Yllanfallen sheet music, the songs I'd had pressed on me by an obliging shopkeeper in Ygranyllon. But while my memory for directions is abysmal (and for lyrics, ditto, to my eternal regret), my memory for melodies — and obscure trivia — is something else.

I began to play *Yshllyn Ara Elenaril* first, but after three notes I changed my mind. Jay wouldn't thank me for raining all over his sandwich, and what self-respecting Brit would ever ruin a rare day's sun? I played *Syllphyllan* instead, a rippling, jaunty piece said to be beloved of sprites. I had not noticed any popping out of the woodwork at Home to admire me and my music, but if we were in — or near — Yllanfallen territory out here, then maybe...

'That's pretty,' said Jay, sandwich-free and rather recumbent. Lucky I didn't choose *Llewellir*. He'd be snoring by now.

I was about to retort — something along the lines of *pretty is as pretty does* — but I felt a faint stirring on the edge of my magickal senses. Something unfurled, like flower petals in the sun. It was the barest whisper of a sense, nothing so profound as an invisible magickal gateway opening. But it felt... familiar.

I played on, until I had gone through my entire repertoire of Yllanfallen songs — including *Llewellir*, Jay would have to take his chances with the soporific melody. I added Addie's song on top, just for luck, and before I had got halfway through its beloved tones Adeline herself appeared again, ears pricked up, pale tail streaming like a banner in the wind, and the pearlescent spiral of her horn glinting in the sun.

Excellent. It wouldn't hurt one's credibility to show up with a unicorn once beloved of an ancient Yllanfallen king. Addie had serious connections.

When at last I ran out of music, I slowly lowered my pipes from my lips and half turned.

There, crouched in the long grass about twelve feet away, was a sprite. She was distinct from the others I had seen in Mum's kingdom: this creature was lovely, a young one perhaps, with smooth, pearly skin touched with sky blue, tumbling pale-gold hair and an intriguing sea-foam gauze dress I really wanted to ask her about. Her eyes were wide and entranced, and she was staring at — Addie.

'Hello,' I said cautiously, and smiled my best smile.

I was prepared for her to dash away, but she did not. She made no movement at all, only stared fixedly at Addie. It was as though I had not spoken at all.

I cleared my throat. 'Um, where do you live?' I tried. 'Aylligranir?'

Her gaze flicked briefly to me as I spoke the kingdom's name, and at once she began to fade, her outline turning misty.

'Wait!' I said. 'Don't go. We aren't here to cause trouble.' On an impulse, I waved my syrinx pipes, letting the pallid skysilver catch the sunlight.

She looked at them, and frowned. 'Had I known it was a *human* playing our songs,' she said, and did not seem minded to finish the sentence. I supposed the implication was clear enough.

'I'm an unusual human,' I said hastily. 'Daughter of Queen Delia of Ygranyllon.' I made her my best curtsey. It hurt a bit to effectively credit Mum with my syrinx pipes, and indeed the presence of Addie in my life, but needs must.

The sprite looked hard at me, and she was no longer entranced. 'And what does Her Majesty of Ygranyllon wish of us?'

'Nothing,' I began.

But Jay, on his feet again, came up beside me, and nudged me powerfully with his elbow. 'We are here as envoys,' he said. 'With messages for Her Majesty, Llirriallon.'

The sprite folded her thin arms. 'Then how is it that you linger here at the gate? Did not Delia, Her Majesty, grant you means of entry?'

'Er, Delia's only just taken the throne,' I said. 'And Ygranyllon was without a ruler for some time, as you may know. We are here to re-establish lost links with Aylligranir.'

The sprite checked out Adeline again, who unwittingly played her part by looking both deeply magickal and wholly unperturbed at hanging around with us.

I wished, briefly, that I had the power to be a unicorn myself outside of the borders of Addie's glade. *That* might impress Miss Suspicious Sprite.

But at length she dropped the prickly attitude, and returned my curtsey. Hers, of course, was infinitely more graceful. 'Doubtless Aylligranir will welcome the envoys of Ygranyllon,' she said.

'Tha—' I began.

'I will go and check,' she said, ignoring me, and disappeared.

7

'As WAITING ROOMS GO,' said Jay, 'This one isn't bad.'
He reposed himself upon the grass once more, shut his
eyes, and apparently dozed off.

I stood watching him for a few minutes, undecided
about whether or not to interrupt his nap. As opportuni-
ties for R&R went, the locale was ideal but the timing was
pretty bad.

But he looked so comfortable lying stretched out in the
verdure, with a tiny half-smile on his sun-bathed face, that
I didn't have the heart.

He didn't seem to mind that he was exhausted, yet expected to soldier on; nor that Milady kept him hopping,
week in, week out. He never complained. Either he loved
the job *that* much, or he had one hell of a work ethic.

Which made me wonder, once again, about the Jay behind the workhorse façade. Though we'd been working together for some weeks now, I was aware that I still didn't know him very well. There had hardly been the time to try. The Jay I knew was tireless, unbelievably dedicated, magickally remarkable, and very self-contained. He'd occasionally got a little irritated with me (my fault, always), but his temper rarely frayed, he never panicked, and he hardly ever worried. A cool cucumber, you might say.

But nobody was like that all the time. Em Rogan had called him "controlled", and she was right. Where was the real Jay, behind the top-of-the-class star student of the Hidden University? What did he care about, besides his studies and his mission with the Society? The only glimpses I'd really had into his inner world were disparate things like his dress sense (that jacket didn't quite go with the image), the motorbike (ditto), and...

Nope, that was about it.

Might have something to do with the family, I mused. The only time I really saw him animated was when he talked about his siblings, of which there were at least three—

'You're staring at me,' said Jay, and I realised with a start that his dark eyes were open.

'Was not,' I said automatically.

'And you had that pensive look on your face.'

'Pensive?' I tried my best smile on him. 'Wasn't thinking anything, I swear.'

'One might even say, inquisitive.' Jay sat up with a slight groan, and brushed grass seeds out of his hair. 'Whatever I've done to deserve such scrutiny, I beg mercy.'

'I was just wondering,' I began, but with a *whoosh* of magick — tasting like clear air after a thunderstorm, and smelling of white wine — our not-so-friendly local sprite was back.

She'd developed a smile.

'My name is—' she said, followed by several unpronounceable syllables I will not attempt to recreate. 'It means *flow of bright water* in your tongue.'

'...Is it all right if we call you that?' I said.

'Maybe just "Flow",' Jay amended.

Flow bowed her assent. 'You are welcome in Aylligranir, Cordelia Vesper and Jay Patel,' she announced. 'Her Majesty is eager to meet the envoys of Queen Delia. If you will follow me?'

Her manner being far more gracious than before, I was somewhat surprised, and a shade uneasy. Obviously, our ruse had succeeded better than I had expected. Hopefully, anyway. That, or this was a counter-ruse, and upon accepting Flow's gracious invitation we were to be thrown into a deep, dark dungeon.

And how was it that she knew our names? I didn't remember telling her mine, let alone Jay's.

'Our fame has preceded us,' I whispered to Jay, as Flow walked, stately and straight-backed, towards the sheer hillside.

'Can't decide if that's a good thing or bad,' Jay muttered.

Neither could I.

Instead of coming to an abrupt halt at the base of the emerald-green hill, Flow wavered like the water whose namesake she was, and vanished.

'Um,' said Jay. 'What do we do?'

I eyed the impenetrable verdure, no less confused. 'When in doubt, follow suit,' I said, and walked after Flow, putting my feet, as best I could, exactly where she had stepped.

It's hard to walk face-first into a slab of rock, so I shut my eyes.

No impact. No grazed nose. I took two steps, then three, then five, and when I still felt free-flowing air around my face I hazarded a glance.

'Oh,' I said, and stopped.

Flow had walked us into the middle of a city. Right into the middle: we stood in the centre of a wide street, paved in pale, silver-touched stone. To my left and right, and all around me, stupendous buildings soared. They were tall, they were graceful, they were pale and interesting, yet touched here and there with bright motes of colour. Star-stone liberally glimmered, everywhere I looked. Pointed arches embraced grand, clear windows bordered in stained glass; engraved pilasters and carved friezes graced every façade.

I heard music: faint, ethereal, enticing. Faerie bells upon a summer breeze.

It reminded me, sharply, of the music I had twice heard Jay draw forth from a piano, or a spinet, and I looked keenly at him.

'What?' he said. 'I can't possibly be more interesting to look at than all of *this*.'

'Nothing. Sorry.' I needed to put a lid on my curiosity. *Jay* wasn't a mystery to solve.

Flow, oblivious alike to our awed wonder and our conversation, floated away down the street. I hurried to catch up. There were not many other Yllanfallen abroad; our footsteps echoed in the quiet, and the distant music teased insistently at me.

Ahead of us loomed a structure of such size and splendour as to put all the rest to shame: a palace, in other words, set in gardens of such verdure, such ethereal beauty, I could have lived there forever.

And as such, I was obliged to stifle an intense desire to turn tail and run away.

We were here on *one* errand: find out what the Yllan-fallen knew about magickal silver, or indeed about Mary or Cicily Werewode, if the two things proved to be connected. But in posing as envoys from my mother, we would now be obliged to *be* envoys from my mother. And who knew what seductive magick this deliriously gorgeous place would work on our senses while we were at it? Aylligranir was like Ygranyllon, only... better. More beautiful. Less wrecked.

I glanced behind me. Jay walked at my left elbow, and several feet behind both of us strolled a pair of Yllanfallen men. They looked innocuous enough at first glance, but something about their demeanour, the matching dark-blue raiment they wore, and the incidental fact that they were armed tipped me off. These were guards. Either Flow had summoned them to keep us in order, or they had fallen in with us once we'd passed through the palace gates.

So much for my stirrings of a plan to sneak away. Not that it would have availed me very much, this time; it's not like Flow wouldn't notice.

No, we would have to brazen it out.

Palaces are never of meagre proportions, and this one was a fair specimen of its kind, in being far too big and improbably convoluted. Once through the soaring double doors, another ten minutes' walking had to be gone through before we at last arrived at an audience chamber. Presumably. Flow liked the palace; I judged this from the dancing gait she'd adopted once inside the pale, cool walls, and the way her sea-foam gown frisked around her legs. She stopped before a tall, narrow door of solid starstone, the stuff gleaming pale and faintly blue even at this early hour, and bestowed upon us a smile of such angelic exaltation I began to wonder who we were to meet. A queen, or a god?

She said nothing, however, only faded away, as she had before: and the starstone door swung slowly open.

No throne-room lay beyond. No grand, imposing chamber of any sort, in fact; more of a salon, sumptuously decorated but surprisingly comfortable. A carpet the colour of rose quartz covered a silvered floor. Matching, gossamer curtains framed the tall, slim window of clear glass overlooking a profusion of yellow rose bushes below. Velvet divans with plump, embroidered cushions and deep armchairs made up the furniture, surrounding a low table of silvery stone.

The room's only occupant was a slim woman seated at a birchwood desk near the window, pen in hand, eyes fixed upon something faraway. Her black hair was bound back in a simple plait, with a ribbon threaded through, and she wore a loose jade-green robe. Her skin was the colour of amber-touched honey. She looked a little out of place in the pale, elegant room; her vivid colouring washed out the delicate tints of the furnishings. In contrast with her, everything looked a little faded.

She did not look up as we entered the salon, nor did she make any sign that she had noticed us.

I paused a moment, uncertain. Would Flow return? Were we not to be introduced? Even the guards did not seem disposed to assist, having taken up positions upon either side of the door — on the outside.

The door had decided no further visitors were required, and quietly closed itself behind us.

When a couple of minutes passed in silence, I finally cleared my throat. 'Um, good morning. We—'

'Oh!' said the lady, and jumped. She looked at us in round-eyed surprise, and dropped her pen. '*Oh,*' she said after a moment. 'The envoys? I had quite lost myself in thought, hadn't I? Please.' She stood up, came towards us with an eager step, and shook my hand heartily, and then Jay's. 'Do tell me your names,' she said. 'I am sure I was told, but I am afraid I was only half listening, and have forgotten.'

I repressed an urge to steal a look at Jay. Was he as con-fused as I? Who exactly had we been delivered to meet? Flow had implied that the queen would receive us, but this vibrant, daydreaming woman surely could not be her.

'Cordelia Vesper, my lady,' I said, with a curtsey. I could have no idea of her title, supposing she possessed one, but it never hurts to be polite.

'Delia's daughter.' It was not a question, more of a statement, and came with a considering look that took in everything about me, from my hair to my shoes.

'Jay Patel,' said Jay, with a trace of diffidence rather unlike him. Had the splendour of Aylligranir and its palace intimidated him? Surely not, after our sojourn at Mandridore.

'Patel,' repeated her ladyship — the queen? She was, if anything, as arrested by Jay's name as by mine, and subjected him to a fresh scrutiny.

Which did not appear to surprise Jay, though it did discomfit him. He endured it in silence, though his jaw clenched.

'Yes,' she said at last, and with one last, keen look, she released Jay from the pressure of her regard, and looked once more at me.

Llirriallon the Gentle, my hat. Welcoming she may be, but something about her was beginning to scare me.

'Now then, what has my sister-queen to say?' said she, confirming once and for all her identity. Did they not *do* pomp and ceremony?

I straightened, as if that would help. 'Erm. Her Majesty, Queen Delia of Ygranyllon, has sent us to— er, to convey her greetings and respects, and—'

'But she has not, has she?' interrupted Queen Llirrial-lon, gently enough, but the words stopped me dead.

'I beg your pardon?' I stammered.

'Two envoys from Ygranyllon arrived not three days ago,' said the queen calmly. 'The business they arrived to transact is already in hand; therefore I cannot imagine why Delia would trouble to send another, and so soon.'

8

Curse it.

Mum's only recently installed upon the throne of Ygranyllon, and having required some days to recover from serious injury incurred during her inauguration as the queen (sort of), I hadn't expected she would have matters so well in hand already as to have sent envoys to neighbouring kingdoms.

Way to go, Mum!

If only it didn't leave us in hot water.

'Erm,' I said, and cast a frantic glance at Jay.

No help there; he was as stymied as I.

Ah well. Talking us out of (and into) various messes was sort of my specialty.

'You aren't wrong,' I said. 'I, er, didn't know about the other envoys.'

The queen glanced behind us. I refused to be so weak as to turn around, but if I had, I'd bet you anything you like I'd have seen the door quietly opening again, and those two guards coming in.

'I'm sorry,' I said quickly. 'We did not mean to lie our way in. Only Flow seemed inclined to evict us, and we really needed to visit.'

I waited, ready any moment to be seized and ripped to bits. But nothing happened. *Hopefully* she did not imagine we were here to harm her. What manner of inept infiltrators would brazenly show up at her front door, and gab their way inside?

'You *are* Delia's daughter,' said the queen. 'The account I received of your arrival coincides with what I have heard. Why, then, are you here, if your mother did not send you?'

'You've heard of me?!'

Faint amusement twinkled in her amber eyes. 'The events that led to your mother's installation as queen were... noteworthy. Such tales spread.'

I wondered what part in that Jay and I were said to have played, and decided not to ask. I could not tell if Queen Llirriallon approved of my mother's ascension to royalty and authority, or whether she shared the opinions of those of her people who despised the prospect of a human ruler. Her composure was too good, her serenity untouched. I *hoped*, though, that the welcoming manner she had shown indicated the former. She'd already known, then, that we were no official envoy.

I realised, too late, that I had not answered her question. Jay pre-empted me.

'We, er, came out of no idle curiosity,' said Jay. 'If you know of us, you must know that we work for The Society for the Preservation of Magickal Heritage. We're here because we are looking for something.'

Right. Honesty is the best policy, etc. I formed my signature sign to back up Jay's words: the Society's three crossed wands, and my own unicorn symbol superimposed over them (how very fitting that choice now seemed). 'We were actually hoping to consult your archivist,' I put in. I debated throwing the word "alchemy" straight in, but dismissed the notion. For one thing, running around asking about alchemy in any serious fashion tends to get a person labelled an eccentric, and I really didn't need any extra help in that department. For another, I wasn't sure what to make of her majesty of Aylligranir. If her people knew something to our benefit, would she be minded to share it, or hide it? I always prefer to speak to fellow scholars, when I can. They're intrigued by tricky questions, and often as desirous of finding answers to an interesting puzzle as I am.

'And any alchemists you may have at the court,' said Jay, reaching totally different conclusions to mine.

Curse it.

'Alchemists?' echoed the queen, her brows going up. 'A discredited art, no?'

'Yes,' I said. 'But nonetheless we have questions for anyone who might have kept it up—'

'There is no such person here,' said the queen, and that keen look was back in her eye. 'What is it that you are looking for?'

Now Jay looked to me, and well he might. What could I possibly say? How top secret was Milady's magickal-modulator project? She had welcomed a partnership with the Court at Mandridore; did that mean she was as happy to draw other fae courts into the scheme?

This was why I hadn't chosen to show our hand. *All* the awkward questions that follow.

Fine, well. Nothing ventured, nothing gained. And did not every fae court, and every magickal society, stand to gain if the Society could pull this off?

'We're after magickal silver,' I said. 'What you call moonsilver, or skysilver — at least, that's what they were calling it in Ygranyllon. We need it in quantity, and as you must know there isn't a great quantity of it to be had. So we're following some rumours. It's said here and there that the alchemists of the past may have sought to create it, and *may* have succeeded, but if they did they've been awfully quiet about it.'

'Such a project, were it successful, must be very lucrative,' said the queen, and I am sure I did not imagine the shade of disapproval in her tone.

'Very,' I said quickly. 'But that isn't why we want to make it.'

'I think you had better tell me the rest,' said the queen.

So we did. Not quite all of the rest, but a lot of it. I began with our first venture into lost Farringale, and ended with Torvaston's abandoned scheme to create a solution via magickal means. 'So if we are here as envoys,' I concluded, 'it is as members of the Society, not of my mother's court. And we are seeking help. To save magick. For everyone.'

It wasn't a bad speech, if I say so myself. Harder to say whether Queen Llirriallon was impressed by it or not; she sat very still, ruminating upon everything we had said, and I could not tell from her face what thoughts were passing through her mind.

Told all in a rush, the way Jay and I had just done, it sounded far-fetched. Crazy. Magickal parasites, lost royal houses, alternate Britains, mysteriously powerful artefacts and two ordinary magicians at the heart of it all: would she believe it? How much of everything we'd said did she already know?

At length, she spoke.

'At court, we have a store of moonsilver.'

My heart leapt, and began to race. Giddy gods, could it be that easy? Would she give her kingdom's store into the Society's care?

'It is not enough for your purpose, but perhaps some token of it may be of use to the Society. I am prepared to offer a loan, via the proper channels of course.'

Of course. She wouldn't just let us waltz off with it, which was fair.

But if it was a loan, she did not intend for it to be used in the creation of any magickal modulator. So, then...?

She read my questions in my face, for she smiled a little, and rang the tiny, silvery bell that stood on a corner of her desk. 'You wanted to speak to an archivist?' she said, and a moment later the door swung open.

'Please take Miss Vesper and Mr. Patel to see Hylldirion,' she said to the green-clad official who entered. 'He is our Lorekeeper,' she said to Jay and I. 'I believe you may find him useful to consult.'

Jay was laughing softly as we exited the queen of Aylligranir's salon.

'What?' I hissed, trailing after our taciturn guide at a distance of a few feet. He'd barely acknowledged us, offering us the scantest of bows before turning his back and walking off. Apparently we were to follow or not, he neither knew nor cared.

'Was that us being *gently* disposed of?' said Jay.

'The classic token-gesture-and-fob-off combo,' I nodded. 'She's a master at it.'

On the face of it, Llirriallon the Gentle had been most obliging and helpful. But Jay and I hadn't missed the fact that she had asked no questions about the modulator, or our quest to rebuild it. She'd made no professions of solidarity, and offered us no real assistance. Just the loan of a small piece of unworked moonsilver, however that was supposed to help, and then dispatched us to pester her Lorekeeper with our questions.

And there'd been that gleam of something in her soft eyes that looked awfully like amusement.

I consoled myself by remembering what Val had said. *The shining lights of history were often considered cranks in their own time.* I had no real problem with being considered a crank. In fact, Milady rather specialised in being underestimated.

Still, it would've been nice to meet with more real assistance, here at an unusually intact Yllanfalen enclave.

A stray thought filtered in.

'Jay,' I said, in a different tone. 'Did she *know* you?' I was thinking of the way she'd stared at Jay, and repeated his surname. And the way everyone seemed to know who we were the moment we showed up, though that might just be because I was notorious for causing a ruckus, and Jay was getting famous by association. That, and for his shiny Waymastery skills.

Jay cast me a glance I can only term shifty. 'Er, no.'

'And now for the truth?' Our green-clad guide walked on at a measured pace, either oblivious or uninterested, and he'd led us through so many twisty corridors I had hopelessly lost what passed for my bearings. Hopefully Jay had some idea of where we were.

With a sigh that expressed the utter futility of trying to fob *me* off, Jay said: 'She doesn't know me. She may know of my family.'

'The Nottinghamshire Patels?' That surprised me. What possible link could there be between Jay's family and an Yllanfalen kingdom in Yorkshire?

'My mother tried to get me admitted for music tutelage,' Jay said. 'She was quite persistent, I understand.'

My thoughts flew to Jay at the piano, and the ethereal music drawn forth by his clever fingers. Music tutelage, or musical magick? 'Did she succeed?'

'No. I was not invited to study here, or at any other Yllanfalen kingdom.'

Some piece was missing in this little history. Jay's musical talents were inarguable, but few parents, however devoted, would have the gumption to importune the Yllanfalen for training. Not least because of its utter futility. These fae had never been especially welcoming of human visitors, however magickal they might be. Even with my links to a fellow Yllanfalen queen, I knew our time in Aylligranir was likely to prove brief; soon enough we would be politely encouraged to take ourselves off.

Why, then, had Mrs. Patel considered it worth the effort to try?

'Is there some reason she thought they might—' I began, but our guide at last stopped in the middle of another interminable corridor, opened a low door set into the pale stone wall, and bowed us through it. 'At the queen's pleasure, Lorekeeper,' he said to whoever was inside.

I walked past him, and stepped into a room Val might literally have killed for. A library, naturally, and not, whatever my words might have suggested, the spectacular kind. Unlike much of the rest of the palace, this room had no soaring ceilings, no pillars and statuary, no starstone or gilding. Its proportions were surprisingly modest, but every inch of the space was turned to the practical purpose of close study. The books crowding the shelves of the many plain oak bookcases were well-used and well-loved, though also well-kept; reading desks and comfortable chairs were tucked into every cranny and corner; handsome glass cases hinted at rare and precious bookly treasures just waiting to spill their secrets. The library was well-stocked, lived-in and loved, and full of the personality of whoever had built it.

Which was, possibly, the gentleman who looked up from a gigantic tome, blinking in befuddled surprise at his unexpected guests. Our guide didn't linger; within moments, the door closed behind us, and Jay and I were left to introduce ourselves to Hylldirion the Lorekeeper.

'Please forgive the intrusion,' I murmured, recognising the bemused, faraway look of a man whose mind was far from the room in which he sat. 'Her Majesty sent us to enquire with you about—'

'Ancestry records? Yes, yes.' Hylldirion set aside his tome — a volume I longed to leaf through, it positively radiated secrets — and stood up. The process cost him some effort, for he looked at least a hundred years old and could easily have been thrice that. He was bald as an egg, his stooped frame clad in a simple blue robe, though his grey eyes held a bright alertness I myself would've envied on many an early morning.

'Later, certainly,' I said, for we did want to pursue the question of the Werewodes and their possible Yllanfalen ancestry. 'But we particularly wanted to ask you about...'

I trailed off, realising that Hylldirion had no way of knowing about the Werewode part of our mission. We hadn't mentioned that to anyone yet, not even the queen.

How then had he known we would be interested in his lineage papers?

'What—' I began, but he was looking at Jay, and Jay had an air of acute embarrassment shaded with irritation, and *he* was most definitely avoiding my eye.

Something slotted into place.

'*Wha*,' I breathed.

Jay's expression turned stony, and an irritated muscle jumped in his jaw. 'We aren't here for that, sir,' he said to the Lorekeeper, with slightly strained politeness.

'*Jay*,' I choked. 'You're— you can't mean that you're—'

It was Hylldirion who answered; Jay maintained his silence. 'Possessed of a degree of Yllanfalen heritage? It's as plain as a pikestaff.'

$$\mathcal{9}$$

IT REALLY WASN'T PLAIN, at least not to my eye. I stared and stared at Jay, and saw the same features as ever. The same *human* features. They were good, no doubt about that: finely etched, sculpted cheekbones, strong jaw, all the hallmarks of what might be considered solid good looks.

But he was human. Not a hint of a fae glamour about him; none of the unusual tints or beautiful, slightly alien cast to the features that might mark him as part fae. None of the things that had stood out so clearly in Cicily Were-wode's portrait.

But the Lorekeeper disagreed. 'You haven't the eyes,' he said to me, not unkindly. 'It's clear enough to me. And to Her Majesty, no doubt.'

'Jay?' I squeaked.

He flashed me a tight, unamused smile. 'Can we talk about it later?'

I folded my arms, and stared him down. No, later wasn't going to be good enough. I'd brought a part-Yllanfalen associate into the middle of an Yllanfalen kingdom, and I had no idea what the political ramifications of that were likely to be. Was he a descendant of someone from Aylligranir? If so, the connection might not precisely please the people here. Was he descended from a scion of a rival kingdom, with whom relations were strained? That could be even worse.

Either way, we'd put ourselves in a difficult position. *Rudeness* didn't begin to cover it; and what if the queen had seen it as an attempt to manipulate or influence her?

Jay needed to tell me stuff like this. Yes, it was personal, but the strictly personal could sometimes have a serious impact upon the professional. And like it or not, I was at present responsible for him.

He rubbed at the back of his neck, not looking at me. He was deeply embarrassed by it, and I wasn't sure why. For all my annoyance, there was nothing actually shameful about his ancestry, and in his case it had clearly benefited him. He'd inherited some part of the legendary Yllanfalen talent for magick-wreathed music.

'My grandmother,' he said shortly. 'Had an — unsanctioned relationship with one of the Yllanfalen. My father was the result.'

He said no more.

That would've been around the 1950s, I thought, or thereabouts. "Unsanctioned" could mean a lot of things, but all of them bad; had it caused a family scandal? Was that why Jay was ashamed of it?

'Do you know who it was?' I said.

He shook his head.

That explained why Jay's mother might have hoped he'd be admitted to music school, though not why he'd been denied. Apparently blood links to the Yllanfalen didn't necessarily count for much with them, either.

I felt a little bad for putting Jay on the spot like that, and offered him an apologetic smile. It was inconvenient — from a professional point of view — that the family didn't know who his ancestor was; it meant I had no means with which to navigate the tricky political waters. Then again, it meant the Yllanfalen might not know, either, which eliminated most of the problems I'd been worried about.

'It may be possible to find out,' said Hylldirion, watching Jay. 'Would you like to know?'

'No,' said Jay shortly, and added, 'Thank you.'

Time to change the subject.

'Anyway,' I said breezily. 'We came to consult you on two primary points, Lorekeeper, if we may.'

Hylldirion sat down again, wheezing softly. He waved a hand, gesturing us to take chairs at will. 'I hope you have brought me an intriguing problem,' he remarked. 'It is a long time since I had a really new idea to dig into.'

That boded well. 'One of them is a mere question of ancestry,' I admitted. 'There was an alchemist in the fourteenth century who may, I suspect, have had Yllanfalen blood herself. I don't know how far back your records go?'

'An alchemist?' he said, and his gaze sharpened upon me. 'What was the name?'

'Mary Werewode. Alternatively her own descendant, Cicily Werewode, about a century and a half later.'

'Werewode.' Hylldirion nodded to himself, and went on nodding. I didn't see what he did, but a fine golden quill pen whisked into the air and sailed off; after a moment I realised it had been caught up and carried away by someone I couldn't see. A sprite, most likely. 'Kindle will find out, if records there are.'

I made a mental note to beware of invisible sprites hovering about. We perhaps ought to have been a bit more discreet with some of the things we'd said about the queen.

Oops.

'Thank you,' I said hastily. 'And the other thing was about alchemy itself. Specifically...' I thought. Specifically what? Specifically, a quick and convenient answer to the complex question of how to produce the most valuable magickal substance known to man or fae? An easy, straightforward recipe for the kind of stuff some people would kill for, just lying on a shelf in the Lorekeeper's library? Hah.

No.

'We, um, wondered if your people might ever have investigated some of the old alchemical pursuits,' I said cautiously.

Hylldirion's eyes twinkled. 'Lead into gold, and the elixir of immortality?'

'No. *Real* alchemy. Magickal alchemy. In particular...'

'Magickal silver,' said Jay, growing impatient with my waffling. 'Moonsilver, as you call it. Or skysilver.'

Hylldirion considered us both in silence, for a moment or two. 'And what leads you to believe that such a thing was ever possible?' he asked. 'Surely all who remember the moonsilver know that it was pulled from the ground, like any other metal.'

'Not quite any other metal,' I said. 'Some are now formed by amalgamation, of course.'

'And you think that might be a way to make moonsilver?' said the Lorekeeper. 'Mix silver with — something, and there it is?'

'No,' I snapped. 'Were it so simple, the world would be awash with the stuff. I have no idea how it might be contrived; I only know that *some* one or two ancient scholars heavily implied that they had done it.'

'Including these Werewodes you spoke of,' said the Lorekeeper.

'Yes. Possibly.'

Hylldirion sat with steepled fingers, his expression unreadable. 'I can see why the search has led you here.'

Was that a glimmer of contempt in his eyes? I bridled at the mere possibility.

'We are not asking for the sake of personal gain,' I said. 'We aren't treasure hunters, if that is what you imagine. We're from the Society, and we're trying to save magick. Moonsilver has the distinction of being peculiarly adept at absorbing magickal energy, and under the right conditions also amplifying it. As such, it is of great interest just now; both to the Society, and to Their Majesties of the Court at Mandridore.'

I hate name-dropping, but sometimes it's necessary. And if there is one fae court that all the others take seriously, it's Mandridore. Pomp, power and influence.

Hylldirion did not respond directly to anything I'd said. He was silent for a while longer, while his lively mind turned over who-knows-what ideas. Then he said: 'I do not know what your sources might be, but one would do

well to ask why the art has fallen so far out of favour —
indeed, been all but forgotten altogether. If there is any
validity to any of those old spells, why are they no longer
practiced? Why are they not respected?'

'We had asked ourselves those same questions,' I allowed.

'And what conclusions did you reach?'

'Either that there *is* no validity to any of it, in which case
we are destined for a great disappointment. Or that they
were unusually adept at maintaining a strict secrecy.'

'Why might they have worked so hard to maintain such
a secrecy, do you think?'

I shrugged. 'Most likely because alchemy has never been
held in very high regard, and no serious scholar likes to be
laughed at for their choice of subject.'

But Hylldirion shook his head. 'No area of endeavour
that can prove its worth ever remains a laughing-stock for
long. *If* alchemy has anything to offer, why was it kept
secret? Why is it still?'

'Because,' said Jay, 'keeping it secret was more important
than giving it to the world. Which means something that
was done with it was — too effective.'

'It may simply be that the alchemists of old were avaricious in the extreme,' said the Lorekeeper, nodding and
relaxing back into his chair. 'After all, of what use would
it be to turn lead into gold, if everyone could do it? Soon

enough, gold would be as common as lead, and therefore as valueless, and the whole procedure rendered worthless.'

'That could well apply to moonsilver,' I said.

Hylldirion nodded. 'It may also be that the procedure proved dangerous in some way, too much so to be worth it. Or that it was too difficult, or too expensive — yes, even if the product was moonsilver. It is a substance of great, but not infinite value.'

These objections I privately waved away. Danger we would risk, for the sake of so important a project, and no expense could possibly be spared considering the importance of the ultimate goal.

'We consider ourselves duly warned,' I said, with a slight smile.

Hylldirion smiled back. 'It was my duty.'

'We understand.'

'We return, then, to the question of *how* so important a secret might have been kept for so long, even at the expense of attracting ridicule. Supposing such a secret exists.'

I couldn't tell if he knew something, and was being cagey for effect, or whether this, too, was an attempt to warn us of impending disappointment.

Lorekeepers. They're as addicted to mysteries as I am.

'If there are books on the subject,' I said, 'they've never been found. At least, not to my knowledge.'

'They might be hidden in some deep, dark pit some-where,' Hylldirion agreed. 'An unusually impenetrable one, that somehow no one has got into in hundreds of years. That is a possibility.'

My thoughts flew to Farringale. Would it be worth an-other trip back, to scour the library for such a book? Could it be possible? It could take weeks on end to search all the books on all those shelves. Even with Mauf's help, I couldn't see it taking much less time. And what if there was nothing there? Weeks of subjection to the dangerously unstable magickal overflows of the place, and maybe noth-ing to show for it.

Not exactly Plan A material.

'Alternatively?' continued the Lorekeeper.

He'd asked a question. I had no idea what he was driving at. 'Um,' I said. 'Perhaps nothing was written down?'

Jay, though, was shaking his head. 'Scholars of every academic discipline write things down. They have to; no-body could remember the half of complex spells or lengthy research without written records, and then it could never be passed on.'

'Perhaps they didn't want to pass it on. Isn't that the point?'

'Not widely, perhaps,' Jay said. 'But to the select few? Nobody wants to feel that their life's work will die when they do. They wrote down whatever they had, I'd bet a year's salary on it.'

'I am inclined to agree,' said the Lorekeeper. He watched us with both faint amusement and a kind of eagerness, like a dedicated teacher painstakingly guiding a pair of befuddled students towards enlightenment.

He couldn't just *tell* us whatever he knew?

Lorekeepers.

'What possibilities remain?' he prompted.

'It was written down,' said Jay, 'but in such a way as to be incomprehensible to the majority.'

I gasped. 'Hidden in plain sight! Like my chamber pot.'

10

Hylldirion looked at me oddly, but Jay snickered. I'd got around the problem of how to store my own valuables by way of misdirection. Instead of having a safe, or a big, fancy chest with a big, inviting lock on it — anything obvious that begged to be investigated by a chancer of a thief — I had a cracked old chamber pot. No one would ever think to look in *there* for something worth stealing.

'Never mind,' I told the Lorekeeper.

Course, if you know the magickal password — so to speak — my shabby old chamber pot miraculously turns back into its true shape: a crystal chest full of goodies.

So if I could protect my valuables by disguising them as a repellent article of no interest to anyone, the alchemists of the past could certainly have protected their own valuable findings by disguising them as inanities — or the ramblings of a madwoman.

My thoughts flew to Cicily Werewode's journal, and Mary Werewode's moonbathing.

'Do you have reason to think that's what was going on?' I looked hard at our new friend the Lorekeeper, who seemed to be enjoying our ignorance far more than I liked.

'What, exactly?' said Hylldirion mildly.

I took a breath. 'That the alchemists of the past, the ones with enough magickal ability to interest us, were using some kind of code to record their findings.'

'It is plausible, is it not?' said the Lorekeeper.

'More so than that nothing has survived at all.'

'Indeed.'

'So, then,' said Jay, leaning forward. 'Was there a universal code, understood among most alchemists, or did each one develop their own?'

'Both,' said Hylldirion. 'Some terms were commonly used. Among regular or non-magickal alchemists, such terms as fool's gold, horn silver, dragon's blood and pearl ash — you will likely have heard some of them, even today. The focus of magickal alchemy, of course, was jewels more than metals; some sought to create such articles as *sun's glow*, which seems to have referred either to sunstone or to diamonds, or *blush of love*, which meant rubies.'

So far, so familiar. I'd learned from my own research that many magicians or witches who practiced alchemy sought to create jewels, though not just any jewels: the magick-wreathed kind from which prized Wands are made. Why do you think I got in so much trouble for losing the Sunstone Wand? (and I did). Those things are not plentiful.

As far as I knew, they'd failed as surely as the likes of Flamel failed at making gold out of lead.

'Some of them, of course, likely had their own terms between smaller groups of researchers,' said Hylldirion. 'On which point, I cannot assist you further. Alchemy was never my area of expertise.' *Or interest,* his tone implied.

Well, few people had ever taken much interest in so batty an art. That was the whole problem.

'Lorekeeper,' I said. 'Is it your opinion that anybody has ever succeeded in producing or creating magickal silver? By transmutation, or something else?'

'I would be very surprised,' he said, without hesitation.

I wanted to ask why, but Jay intervened with a question of his own. 'What *is* magickal silver?' he said. 'Is it literally silver, or not?'

That was a good question, one I had briefly explored but been unable to answer. Our library, at least, had little to offer on the subject. The stuff had, perhaps, never been prevalent enough, at least in our Britain, to merit much study. Or perhaps its potential had never really been understood.

'It is not silver,' said the Lorekeeper. 'In terms of its physical make-up it has little in common with *real* silver. It is only silver-coloured. What is it made from? How is it formed? These questions I cannot answer. I do not know that anybody can. The alchemists of old termed it a distillation of the elements of air and water, which may go some way towards explaining the names the Yllanfalen have historically used. That, of course, is a discredited notion these days.'

Yes, the world has moved on from the idea that the four elements have much to do with anything, even in magick. But that didn't necessarily mean there was not a kernel of truth lurking somewhere in there.

I filed the idea away.

'Regarding jewels,' I offered. 'I understand the ones *we* value to be identical in composition to any other, only they are said to form in areas of great magickal intensity, and thus absorb a degree of it before they are extracted. This seems to be a widely accepted explanation. But if magickal silver is *not* silver, then I suppose the same can't be true.'

Hylldirion spread his hands. 'Perhaps not. Perhaps yes, and some aspect of that process of absorption has a transformative effect on the base metal. Who can say? Without extensive study, we must rely on speculation, and such studies have never been conducted.'

I sighed, beginning to feel dejected. Here in the heart of Yllanfalen power, I had hoped to uncover some genuine insights; they, after all, were the one people I knew to have incorporated their *moonsilver* quite deeply into their culture. But it seemed the Queen's Lorekeeper knew little more than we did.

Still, the clue about the code was of use. I'd send that snippet of information to Val at my earliest opportunity, and see what she made of it.

A scroll drifted past Hylldirion's head, wandered off to the far side of the library, and then came back again.

'Thank you,' said the Lorekeeper, accepting and unfurling it. A slender thing when rolled up, it went on and on and *on* when unrolled, comprising far more parchment than seemed possible. I watched in dumbfounded silence as Hylldirion browsed through several reams of it.

'Werewode, was it not?' he murmured, without looking up.

'Mary Werewode, in the late thirteen hundreds,' I confirmed. 'And Cicily Werewode, who married, at my guess, somewhere in the fifteen-eighties.'

'There would not be a marriage record,' said Hylldirion. 'Because there would not be a marriage, or certainly not a sanctioned one. Not at that time. If your Mary or Cicily were born of a union between one of my people and one of yours, it would have been an illicit one.'

I felt disappointment again. 'So you will have no way of knowing?'

'Well.' Hylldirion paused in his perusal of the scroll. 'If there was a birth, and presumably there must have been, that might have been a matter of record. And here we are.' He laid the paper, very carefully, over the surface of his desk.

Jay and I leaned over it.

In tiny, crabbed scrawl I read: *Margaret Werewode*, and the date 1538.

Cicily's mother? It had to be. The timing was perfect.

'So Mary was probably human but Cicily only partially so,' I said, excitement rising again. 'I knew it!'

'What is that scroll?' said Jay, in a tone that made me look quickly at him. He was unreadable, but I saw a certain tension in him.

The Lorekeeper said calmly: 'It is a register of all children born to Yllanfalen and human pairings.'

I stared at the endless scroll, aghast. 'But it goes on forever.'

'The records date back rather more than a thousand years.'

'Oh! A mere nothing.'

Jay did not speak. Looking at him again, I could guess at his thoughts, even if they did not show on his face. Somewhere on that scroll, his father's name must be written — and, presumably, the name of his Yllanfalen grandfather.

Would he ask? I waited, giving him time to decide.

He said nothing.

The name of Cicily's grandfather was there: Igryr of Everynden. 'What is Everynden?' I asked, pointing at the entry.

'It is one of the towns of Aylligranir.'

I nodded, thinking. So Cicily was part Yllanfalen; was that why she had taken such an interest in her great-great-grandmother's work? Had she inherited the Yllanfalen fascination with magickal silver?

That did not altogether follow, by itself. I began to wonder how much she had known her grandfather, this Igryr of Everynden — and whether he had shown her anything. Given her anything.

Something precious and rare, for the granddaughter he should not have had. An heirloom. A silvery one.

It wasn't so far-fetched. Magickal silver had never been plentiful, but five hundred years ago it had been somewhat more so than it was today. A Curiosity or a small Artefact made from magickal silver, given into her care by her mysterious and magickal ancestor? *That* would kick off a strong interest in the substance, no doubt; especially if she could also connect it with her great-grandmother's journals.

Who would have it now?

If anyone, the Elvyngs.

'One last question,' I said to Hylldirion. 'You haven't got any famous magickal alchemists in your kingdom's history, by any chance?'

'I should think it highly improbable that anybody would have thought it worth their while to bother,' said the Lorekeeper.

That response rather took me aback. 'Why do you think that?'

'Because...' The Lorekeeper looked thoughtfully at me, then at Jay, apparently struggling with a decision of some kind. 'There would have been no need,' he said finally. 'There are several instances of powerful artefacts wrought from moonsilver holding a high place in the culture of some one or other of the Yllanfalen kingdoms, and that is not a coincidence. Our culture has historically prized the silver most highly, for its beauty and its properties. And we were able to do so because we had what was once a significant source. The Moonsilver Mines were once the property of all of the Yllanfalen monarchs, until they ran dry of silver in the late fourteenth century. They have been of little interest to anyone, since.'

Something about his demeanour tipped me off: there was more.

'Just where were those mines?' said Jay, glancing at me.

Hylldirion smiled. 'Everynden.'

11

'We need to go back to the Elvyngs,' I said to Jay perhaps half an hour later, when we were once more on the
right side — the human side — of the boundary between
Yorkshire and Aylligranir. 'Bet you a year's salary Cicily
had some moonsilver paraphernalia from her father, and
another year's salary the Elvyngs have hung onto it.'

'No bet,' said Jay. 'It's too obvious.'

He offered nothing else, only walked along beside me,
collar turned up against the drizzle of summer rain that
now watered the hillside. He'd been quiet ever since our
first introduction to the queen, and remained so now.

I'd had to wrestle with myself. I'd been so tempted to excuse myself on some small pretext, dash back to the library
and find out who Jay's Yllanfalen grandfather was. I told
myself I'd be doing it for him: that I could, someday when

he changed his mind, hand him the answer to this family puzzle. He would be pleased. Right?

But that wasn't the real reason I was tempted, or it wasn't the whole reason. My cursed curiosity had got hold of that little mystery and refused to let go.

And I didn't quite understand Jay's thinking. How could he not want to know? How could he be within seconds of finding out who he was, and pass it up?

The man puzzled me. Exceedingly.

I took out my phone, by way of distracting myself, and typed furiously. Val needed to know everything we'd learned, and quickly.

I ended with:

Hoping we have a cryptographer at Home?

I got a response within seconds, the prompt buzzing of my phone making me jump.

Val said: *Yes. Also we have Crystobel Elvyng at Home.*

'Whaaaat,' I gasped, and showed Jay. 'Quick, Whirly Wizard. To the library!'

'I know this is going to sound weird,' he said. 'Coming from me, that is, instead of you. But do you suppose we could eat first?'

'Note to self,' I said, looking uselessly around at the rolling hillside notably unadorned with cafe or shop. 'Do not starve the Waymaster. Erm, you don't happen to know of a village hereabouts, do you?'

Jay merely pointed.

'Right.' I set off down the hill in the direction indicated, heading for cake and glory, and Jay trudged manfully along beside me.

WE WERE NOT MUCH more than an hour delayed before we reached home. I'd stuffed Jay with a stack of sandwiches and scones and myself with a piece of cake — just the one, I occasionally have *some* sense of proportion I swear — and thus revived, he'd managed the return trip smoothly enough. We emerged in the preserved henge in the cellar at Home, and I clattered straight up the stairs.

Jay followed at a more sedate — weary? — pace. As such, I had thirty whole seconds to stare my fill at Crystobel Elvyng before he caught up with me.

She was seated in the library with Val. *Not* languishing in front of the head librarian's big, imposing desk, the way most of us do. The matriarch of the Elvyng dynasty merited the red carpet treatment. There's a handsome fireplace with a brick surround in the main hall of the library, flanked by a pair of silver brocade chairs. I don't think I have ever seen a fire lit in that hearth; there is no earthly way Val would risk the books like that, however cold it may be. I have never seen the chairs used, either.

Until today. Val had taken possession of one, and her august guest sat at her ease in the other.

I received a peculiar impression of there being a third presence in the room, which was probably House. The building mostly leaves us to get on with things, but once in a while it takes an interest.

I couldn't blame it for taking an interest in Crystobel Elvyng. She's about my age, or only a little older; mid-thirties at the most. She has all the poise of a much older woman, though. In pictures she tends to appear exquisitely well-dressed, and positively oozes confidence.

Comes of growing up entrenched in privilege, I suppose. She'd been an Elvyng since the moment of her birth, and in the magickal world, they're the next best thing to royalty. Better, in some ways.

It's a matter of power. They're all remarkably well-endowed with it (though as a minor point of interest, they have yet to produce a Waymaster). They are also incredibly rich, of course. In what world will the perfect mix of wealth and power *not* confer fame and glory upon the wielder? Not this one, anyway.

For my part, I have a horrible fascination with their entire lifestyle. Which puts me on a par with most of the rest of magickal Britain, I suppose.

After years of admiring her from afar, now I beheld Crystobel Elvyng relaxing in the best chair in Val's library, and I did not know what to think. If she could only have managed to be ordinary looking, she might be more believable as a real, breathing human like the rest of us. But of course, she isn't. Whether Cicily's Yllanfalen heritage has bred true down the centuries, or whether she is just lucky, she has excellent features, clear skin the colour of peaches in milk, and a wealth of honey-brown hair. On that day, she was wearing a cerulean velvet coat I might cheerfully have killed for, and boots to match.

Jay came up behind me while I was taking in this scene, and having devoted about three seconds to his own observations, he whispered in my ear: 'Crushing on Crystobel?'

'That or experiencing an unjustified and irrational resentment,' I whispered back. 'Cannot currently decide which.'

'They're just people,' he said. 'Like you and me.'

'That's not what the papers say.'

Jay raised a brow. 'Since when do you care what the papers say?'

'I don't *care*, exactly. But it's difficult to help being a little bit influenced. I feel like we're in the presence of a minor goddess, and I cannot decide whether she deserves all that reverence.'

'Nobody does. Problem solved.' Jay flashed me a quick smile, and moved past me into the library.

Val looked up. 'Aha, Jay — Ves with you?'

'Here,' I said, stepping forward with what I hoped was my usual insouciant manner. I didn't want to feel self-conscious just because we had a celebrity in the House. I'd managed not to be too much of an idiot when I'd met Baron Alban; why was Crystobel Elvyng different?

Because you identify with Crystobel in ways you never had to with Alban.

She was too much like me, while also being incredibly, impossibly different.

But she was smiling at both of us, and either she was an excellent actress or she was genuinely pleased to meet us. I refused to speculate as to which it was.

Introductions over, Crystobel looked keenly at Jay and me in turn, and said: 'I understand you are interested in one of our ancestors.'

The royal "we", I thought, and mentally kicked myself.

'Cicily Werewode-Elvyng,' I confirmed. 'Did you know she was part Yllanfalen?'

She raised her brows at that. 'Of course. Some of our family's most celebrated abilities are attributed to that lineage.'

If that were true, I wondered why Cicily's portrait had been stuffed out of sight in a disused garret bedroom in her own gorgeous manor house. Considering I had been wandering around up there without permission or supervision, it was impossible to ask.

I thought, though, of Hylldirion's long, long list of Yllanfalen-human children, and wondered.

'I don't suppose you have any more of Cicily's writings among your family's papers?' I asked. Val had probably already posed the question, but I had no way of knowing that for certain. Had she told Crystobel what, in particular, we were looking for, or why we were interested? I hoped not. I didn't mind sharing those details with the queen of Aylligranir, but the Elvyngs had... different priorities.

'I'm afraid not,' said Crystobel, with a gentle smile. 'Unfortunately, little of Cicily's life has survived. We have a few letters of hers, which I have given into your librarian's care, but they do not discuss much of any great importance. I would not like to raise your expectations falsely.'

I glanced at Val, who minutely shook her head. The letters contained nothing relevant.

Curse it.

But I was intrigued. How was it that Cicily's possessions had been lost? And in that case, how had that single book of Cicily's ended up in the York archives?

Was Crystobel telling the truth? I had no reason to think otherwise.

Still…

'May I ask why Cicily is of interest to the Society?' said Crystobel, still with that pleasant smile.

I looked at Val. She hadn't spilt the beans, then, and I did not want to.

'We will be at greater liberty to discuss that once our ideas receive some confirmation,' said Val, smoothly but firmly. 'At present we are only speculating.'

Crystobel nodded, but then said: 'Is it about the *argent*? If so, I feel I must give you fair warning. Cicily's work, while interesting, was unrealised at the time of her death.'

'Argent?' repeated Val.

'It has had a few names down the years, hasn't it?' said Crystobel. 'The Yllanfalen call it, I believe, moonsilver?'

It figured she'd know something of it, what with the family link.

Crystobel went on. 'I would be sorry to see so vital an organisation as the Society waste your valuable time on a wild goose chase, so I feel bound to add: there is nothing in alchemy to permit the manufacture of the substance known variously as argent, or moonsilver.'

'Thank you for the warning,' said Val, when neither Jay nor I said anything.

Crystobel evidently considered this the close of the interview, for with her ever-present smile, she got up from the best chair in the library and held out her hand to me.

I took it, and shook it. She had a good handshake: brisk, but not perfunctory. Business-like, without feeling impersonal.

She was almost a foot taller than me. I looked up at her, conscious of a few wistful feelings, and one or two others.

Crush, Jay's voice echoed in my head, and maybe he was a tiny bit right.

'Thank you for your time,' I heard myself say, and a smile — hopefully not a grimace — did something to my face.

'It was my pleasure,' murmured Crystobel.

A few moments later, having taken similarly gracious leave of Val and Jay, Crystobel Elvyng was gone.

12

I EXCHANGED LOOKS WITH both my colleagues, still too busy processing whatever my thoughts might be to say much.

'Well,' said Val after a while.

'Mm,' said I. 'Why was she here?'

'I sent a request for info,' said Val. 'To her secretary. I didn't particularly expect an answer.'

But Crystobel Elvyng herself had responded, with an in-person visit. Prompted by what? Graciousness? Respect for the Society's work?

Could be anything.

'What did *you* think, House?' I said.

I waited, but no real response came. If House had formed an opinion either of Crystobel herself, or of anything she had said, it wasn't sharing.

'I have one question,' said Jay. 'Why was she calling it *argent*? Where did that name come from?'

I nodded. 'Curious to hear a brand-new name for the stuff, from someone who claims to have no special information about it.'

'To be fair, she didn't say that she *had* no special knowledge,' said Val. 'Only that Cicily's work was a dead end.'

'Truth or lie?'

Val shrugged. 'I don't know.'

A gut feeling socked me in the innards. *Truth.*

Oof.

'House thinks she was speaking the truth,' I said, though I did not need to. Judging from the looks on Val's and Jay's faces, they'd both felt the same thing I had.

'Thanks, House,' said Jay weakly.

The door creaked.

'So it's a dead end?' I said, frustration rising. Curse it, weeks of research followed by days of gadding about and it was all a wild goose chase?

'Maybe,' said Val slowly. 'Maybe not.' She sat tapping the end of a pen against her pursed lips, eyes faraway.

I knew better than to interrupt when Val was thinking.

'Chair,' she said at last, quite politely.

Her new, spring-green chair obediently extracted itself from behind her desk and sailed over. She transferred into it and floated slowly away, heading for the nearest wall-to-wall bank of shelves. Not to retrieve any books, it seemed, but merely to stare at them. Some people derive comfort and clarity from long walks in the fresh air, or a stiff drink, or a cake (guilty). Val gets those things from being near her books. I watched as she stretched out one hand, and ran her fingertips gently over the spines of several precious, beautiful old tomes. 'Argent,' she said.

'Argentein,' I said.

'Moonsilver and moon-bathing,' added Jay.

Val's chair spun around so fast I feared she might fall out. 'Yes,' she said. 'There are patterns. Links. The moon, and argent. The Yllanfalen. The Werewodes. *Werewode*, not Elvyng.'

'Maybe Cicily's marriage is incidental,' I agreed. 'Hell, maybe her Yllanfalen father is irrelevant, moonsilver notwithstanding. Maybe this has been a Werewode party all along.'

Val looked hard at me. 'But then, where are Cicily's writings? Or Mary's? Why has so little of either of their work survived?'

'Thought,' said Jay, a touch diffidently.

'You don't need permission to speak, Jay,' I told him. 'This isn't school.'

He merely flickered a brow at that. I hoped the fleeting expression didn't mean he thought I was an idiot for pointing it out. 'Crystobel said that the Elvyngs have little that belonged to Cicily, right?'

'Right.'

'And we've failed to find any further trace of the Were-wode name ourselves. Not in this library, not in the Magickal Archives of the City of York, not in the library of Aylligranir.'

'Right?' I struggled to see where Jay was going.

'And from what Crystobel's words *implied*, they've probably already scoured the rest of the magickal archives worth their salt and found nothing either. And they'd have been thorough, with such a prize on offer.'

'So you're saying there's nothing to find?'

'No. Well,' he amended, 'that could be the case. But think a second, Ves. What do most Society agents spend at least half our time doing?'

'Retrieving artefacts,' I said promptly.

'From where?'

'Jay, could you please just spit it out?' I was beginning to feel like I was taking some kind of exam, and without much hope of passing.

'The chalice we fished out of a museum in Wales,' he said obscurely. 'It's a piece of magickal history lost in the non-magickal world. And there's oceans of it still out there somewhere, waiting to be discovered. We are bringing it all in, one piece at a time — as we discover where they are.'

I straightened, electrified. 'Giddy gods. You mean Cicily's journal—'

'Might have been fished up out of some estate auction or library sale and ended up in the York Archives,' he said, nodding.

'While the rest of her books haven't been!'

'Right! If they exist, maybe they're lying on the shelves in some *ordinary* library.'

'Why, though?' said Val. 'Why wouldn't the Elvyngs have kept her work?'

'The long-ago Elvyngs of the fifteen and sixteen hundreds?' I said. 'If they did not respect her work — and they certainly wouldn't have if she was writing it in absurd-sounding code — then why would her descendants keep it?'

'Or,' said Jay. 'Cicily wanted to hide it from those she feared might abuse it, and gave her books away herself.'

I beamed at him. 'Oh, Jay, is that your first conspiracy theory? I am so proud of you.'

He grinned back. 'Your inspiring influence is paying off.'

I bowed, chuffed to bits. He was really coming along.

'Anyway,' said Val sternly, though I definitely saw a glimmer of amusement. 'You may be onto something, Jay. If Cicily thought she had something significant, but did not want her husband's family to have it, she might have bequeathed her personal effects to her nearest relative in the Werewode line.'

'Ooh,' I said. 'Okay, so, we find out about the Werewodes' other descendants and maybe we can trace those books?'

'Maybe they're all together,' said Jay hopefully. 'Cicily seems to have had access to at least one of Mary's journals. Maybe she had more.'

I bounced a bit on my toes. 'I love a good breakthrough!'

'Get going on it,' said Val to the two of us. 'Me, I am going to see what I can find about this *argent* business. And maybe that Argentein fellow too.'

HAVE YOU EVER TRIED to trace your family history? If you have, you'll know the procedure has certain limitations.

History's rather big, and seven hundred years is a *really* long time. Captain Obvious, I know, but the relative numbers of written records that have survived from as far back as the fourteenth century are minimal. Time does terrible things to organic substances. Also, a lack of cohesive and centralised social structures in those earlier eras meant that many of the records we now take for granted — births, deaths, etc — were never created in the first place.

For these reasons, Jay and I soon gave up on tracing Mary Werewode's line. The only reason we knew her for an ancestor of Cicily's at all was because Cicily wrote about it — in the one book of hers we've managed to find. Tracking down any more of Mary's descendants quickly proved futile.

Cicily Werewode isn't that much better. She may have lived two hundred years later than her batshit crazy great-great-grandmother, but that didn't help us a great deal either. We aren't exactly overwhelmed with surviving papers from the sixteenth century.

We ended up scouring twentieth-century death records for anyone of the name of Werewode who'd died in the Yorkshire area in the past century or so. The idea was to track *those* people's lines back as far as possible, and so on, which is damnably imprecise. After all, people can move a long, long way in five hundred years; the descendants of Cicily's own parents or siblings could be far from Yorkshire by now. They could be on the other side of the world.

We did not get very far, for the simple reason that the Werewode family seems to have died out.

'No one of that name,' I regretfully concluded, after trying every variant I could think of (Werewood, Wherewode,

Weirwode, and so on) in every online records depository I know of.

'They're all dead?' said Jay. 'Is that what that means?'

'It could mean that the line has died out somewhere in the past five hundred years,' I answered. 'It could also mean that the name changed somewhere in that time. If Cicily had a brother, for example, he might have married and had long issue, all with the Werewode name. But if she only had a sister, that sister might also have married and had long issue, but under her husband's name.'

'Which we can't find,' Jay said. 'Because there are no records about Cicily's life back in fifteen-something.'

I looked at him. 'You weren't under the impression this might be easy, were you?'

'I got a little excited,' he admitted. 'Back there when we were brainstorming. It seemed like we were within a stone's throw of an answer.'

'It always does, when you get a bright idea. Then you have to do the grunt work.' I closed down the thirty or so browser tabs I had open, and pushed my chair back from the computer. We were holed up in a study nook in one of the library's antechambers, alone thankfully, with all the firepower that a fast internet connection could give us. Nonetheless, we were getting nowhere. I'd have to rethink.

'Is it always like this?' said Jay.

'What? Library missions? Pretty much. I could easily spend a week digging through the internet looking for this one family line, and end up with nothing. That's how it goes. Lots of dead ends.'

Jay muttered something, of which I distinguished the words *drive me crazy.*

I grinned. 'It can drive me a bit crazy too, eventually, which is probably why I've ended up doing field work most of the time. But on the plus side, there's little to compare to the thrill of suddenly finding your answer, against all the odds, buried in some obscure document at the bottom of some forgotten archive. That, I believe, is what keeps Val going. And she's tireless. If anyone can trace the real Valentine Argentein, it's her.'

Jay nodded along like a man but partially convinced. 'Where does that leave us?' he said. 'We're stopping?'

'Yes. I don't really want to sink a week into this project. That kind of time, we'd have to be pretty sure of finding the answers we want. And we aren't. I mean, it's still quite possible that Mary Werewode was just crazy and Cicily was just deluded. Crystobel Elvyng could be absolutely right: we're on a wild goose chase.'

'You obviously don't think so.'

'It would be fairer to say I'm *hoping* not. But I'm influenced by Val's instincts here. If *she* thinks there's something worth digging for, I'd bet you my rainbow crystal chest that she's right. Do you have any idea what kind of track record she has with this stuff?'

'An impressive one.'

'To say the least. Nonetheless, this isn't really my forte anymore, and it certainly isn't yours. There has to be a better way to find what we're after.' I sat and thought.

So did Jay.

Nothing bubbled up.

'Right, let's think about it another way,' I said. 'Role-play. We're Cicily Werewode. We've spent a lifetime raising Elvyng children and secretly studying alchemy in our spare time. Our husband never took our work seriously so we soon stopped talking to him about it. And when we finally discovered something of value — something that made it *real* — we could have gone crowing in triumph to our doubting marital relatives and showed them what we'd done, but maybe we had some lingering resentment for their failure to support us before—'

'And their distrust of our Yllanfalen heritage,' Jay put in. 'We've had to behave like a proper human lady magician and not pursue projects more befitting of strange fae magick, and that was terribly unfair. They don't *deserve* to have what we've found. And they'd only milk it for cash if they did.'

I waited a moment until I was sure Jay had finished, watching him slightly wild-eyed. He was really getting into that part. I wondered fleetingly if his father had experienced any of that kind of distrust over his half-fae blood. 'Right,' I said. 'So we've decided to hide it from them, and we do that successfully for... some time. Then what?'

'We decide to hide our journals and records by giving them to our trusted relatives.'

'Why? Was the work finished? That doesn't strike me as a project that would ever be quite done with. There would always be something else to research, something new to try. It's a life's work kind of project.'

'Deathbed, then,' said Jay. 'We're dying. We need someone to bequeath our "silly, womanly scrawl" to. We want to make sure they go beyond the reach of the Elvyngs, but without exciting their suspicion or evoking their avarice.'

'We can't bequeath them to our children because they are all Elvyngs. So we choose... a niece, perhaps. Emily Werewode, beloved daughter of our brother George, to whom we have always been close, and who always expressed a flattering interest in everything we did—' I stopped. 'Would we though? Jay, who else was close to Cicily and beyond the reach of the Elvyngs?'

Jay thought. 'Her father? And any other Yllanfalen relatives she may have had on his side?'

'Could've been them.'

'But— but there was nothing about her, or written by her, in the library at Aylligranir.'

'*Probably* nothing, but even if the Lorekeeper was telling the truth about that, it's not decisive. It's the palace library, doubtless the best library in the kingdom, but Cicily wouldn't have left her books to the monarch. She'd have left them to her father, or — or a half-sibling of her own.'

'And they came from Everynden,' said Jay slowly. 'The location of the fabled Moonsilver Mines, but which were long since empty by then.'

'Her father might have been very interested in her work. Could even have helped her with it.'

'Then why didn't she mention him in her journal? She wrote only about Mary Werewode's work.'

'Maybe she didn't know her father yet, at the age of twenty. Maybe she hadn't yet shared her work with him. Maybe she just didn't want to write about him — or she did, but she did it in a code we haven't yet deciphered. Could be anything. We'll probably never know.'

'Great,' said Jay, sagging in his chair. 'I'm calling this the Case of the Endless Dead Ends.'

'It's not a dead end!' I said. 'We can't guess who she left her books to because it could have gone either way; human relatives or Yllanfalen. But we might be able to find out.'

13

'YOU THINK THERE'S A surviving will?' Jay's voice oozed scepticism.

'There could be. There really could be. People's wills are a *great* source of historical info, especially from the early modern period. It's the one kind of document anyone with any property at all would create, and since they were important they tended to be cared for. Lots of last-will-and-testaments have survived, relatively speaking. And Cicily was an Elvyng. We know *that* family line has survived, and if they've managed to hang on to the same *house* all these centuries, surely they've hung onto a lot of family papers too.'

Jay began to look revived. And thoughtful.

'The difficulty is getting hold of them,' I said. 'I already conducted a search of the Academy's attics and didn't find anything like that.'

'Attics?' said Jay, and the scepticism was back.

No, not scepticism. Exasperation.

'Why would they keep papers like that in an attic?' said Jay.

I shrugged. 'Lots of old families don't really value that kind of thing, or they just don't really know what they have. A lot of it gets passed down in boxes, and it goes in the attic with the rest of grandma's stuff that you don't know what to do with but feel too guilty to throw out.'

'Likely true,' said Jay. 'But this is the Elvyng family. They know the value of *everything*.'

'Point,' I conceded.

'There's an archive in the cellar,' he continued. 'It's a repository for all the records, documents and so on pertaining to the academy's history and its students — you know the kind of thing. But since it's specially designed to keep fragile paperwork from succumbing to the ravages of time — and since this is the fabulously wealthy *Elvyngs* and they have stuff like that book box I'd still give my left arm for — I think they know how to keep old documents intact.'

I felt a rising excitement — and a commensurate puzzlement. 'Totally conceivable that they'd have ancient family papers somewhere in there, I grant you, and you're a genius. One question, though. How the hell do you know all that?'

'I'm alumni.'

'You... studied there?'

Jay inclined his head. He had the grace to look faintly abashed. 'Um, they have the best musical programme in the country... I did a six-year stint there before the University.'

I swallowed my envy with only a little difficulty. 'Excellent,' I managed. 'Sometime you should tell me every single detail about what that was like, but in the meantime: how do we extract paperwork from this mythical archive?'

'Easy,' said Jay. He'd taken something out of his wallet while he spoke, and now waved it around. I gathered that it was an Elvyng Alumni card of some sort. 'I'll submit a research request.'

'You can do that?'

Jay nodded, already pushing me out of the way of the computer. 'This doubles as a library card.'

And back came the envy.

WE HAD AN ANSWER far more quickly than I'd dared to hope. Jay's request was processed within an hour, and when he opened up the email he found it contained an attachment.

'Dear Mr. Patel,' Jay read. 'Your request for yada yada has been received, blah blah... ah! They've found it.'

He opened the attachment, and up came a scanned facsimile of Cicily Werewode's last will and testament.

The document was in surprisingly good shape considering it was five hundred years old. Testament to the Elvyngs' magickal conveniences, no doubt. But since it was written in tiny, crabbed script, it bordered upon illegible.

'We're going to need Val for this,' said I.

'She has a plus one buff to Deciphering?' Jay said.

The only response I could offer was a blank look. 'What?'

'It's a gaming joke — never mind.'

'It's just the effect of long, *long* practice.'

'Rude,' said Jay as I forwarded the email to Val. 'She's not much older than you.'

'I know, but she's spent every minute of her Society career in the library, nosing through old documents.'

'While you've spent yours...?'

'Heroically swiping artefacts of indescribable value from the hands of the unworthy.' We were en route by then, heading away from our cosy study carrel back to Val's desk.

Where, of course, she was. As always. 'Val! Check your email.'

Val ceased her perusal of an unidentifiable tome of some antiquity, and glowered at us. She'd surrounded herself with stacks of books tall enough almost to obscure her entirely. 'I don't *do* email when I am reading.'

'I know, but you'll want to see this one right away. Promise.' I couldn't sit and wait for her to read it; I was too excited. I stood instead, barely suppressing the impulse to bounce on my toes. Nervous energy does that to me. What would the will say? Would it hold the answers we needed? It *had* to. I was getting heartily sick of going in circles.

Val closed her tome, carefully and grudgingly, and re-moved her reading spectacles. Once she had her phone in hand and our email on her screen, though, her attitude changed in a flash. As I'd known it would. 'Her *will*?' she said, looking sharply at me. 'Ves, you sorceress of mystery, how did you get this?'

'Nothing to do with me,' I said, pointing at the Jay who was trying to skulk unnoticed behind me. 'Seems we have an Elvyng Academy alumnus among us.'

'I didn't know that,' said Val. 'Why didn't I know that?'

'He appears to be embarrassed by it,' I said, but Val wasn't listening. Cicily Werewode's will had absorbed her utterly.

'I'm not *embarrassed*,' Jay muttered.

'No? With your personal history, most people would have the town crier out about it. Fae ancestry *and* the most prestigious school of magick in Britain on your CV?'

'Thank you for appreciating that I'm not an obnoxious prat.'

'No. Incredibly, scarily hard-working, though. When did you have time for games?'

'Somewhere between two and three in the morning, when my eyes were bleeding too much to read any more.'

'Most people would consider that a good time to go to sleep.'

'At the risk of sounding like said obnoxious prat, most people didn't go to the Elvyng Academy.'

'Touché.' I saluted.

'I— didn't mean to cast aspersions upon your work ethic—' Jay backpedalled furiously.

'And I am mortally offended, but I'll forgive you purely for using the phrase *cast aspersions upon.*'

'Hush,' said Val absently.

We hushed.

About three minutes later, she looked up. 'I don't understand,' she said, and looked back at her phone, as though the words of the will might have changed in those few seconds. 'Cicily left all her worldly possessions to her son, Godfrey Elvyng.'

'That's it?' I caught myself leaning over the desk to get a look at the phone, as though it might say something else if *I* took a look at it.

'That's it,' said Val. 'No sign in here that she had any other children, or siblings either.'

'No mention of her father or grandfather either?'

'Not a one.'

'Well,' I said numbly. 'Curse it.'

There went our theory.

'She could still have given her books to a relative, before she died,' Jay said. 'Maybe not so close as a sibling. A cousin?'

'Could have,' I sighed, sinking into a chair. 'But if she did, it's of no use to us. We've no way to find them.'

'Or her father.'

'Ditto.'

'Well, but,' said Val. She'd put the phone down, and now stared instead at a point some way over my head. I recognised her thinking face. 'What if she didn't?'

'Didn't what?'

'Give away her books. What if she didn't have any other relatives, just the Elvyngs? What if her son *did* inherit everything — including her work on alchemy?'

I sat up a bit, thinking. 'The family might not have kept her journals, if they didn't know there was anything valuable in them.'

'What if they did?'

I blinked. 'What?'

'Listen. With the academic species of mystery, you run into a lot of dead ends. Sometimes it's just ill luck; there really isn't a paper trail to wherever you're trying to go. But sometimes, it means you've taken a wrong turn somewhere. Consider. We concluded that the Elvyngs never took Cicily's work seriously, or that they never knew about it at all. And that supposition sent us off looking for the other people in her life. But what if we were wrong?'

'They knew?' said Jay. 'Her son knew?'

'What she was doing, and that it had value. Yes. He might even have helped her, for all we know. So he inherited all of her possessions; what happened then?'

'Then— then the Elvyngs had the secret of the argent,' I said.

'*If* Cicily succeeded, yes. They at least had whatever progress she had made by the time of her death, and could have built on it afterwards.'

'You're suggesting they've had this secret since at least, what, the early seventeenth century.'

'They might have. How do we know otherwise?'

'We don't. We— why would they hide the fact? Why wouldn't they shout it from the rafters?'

Val's smile was a bit twisted. 'Capitalism?'

I thought about the Elvyng Emporium, and its stock of indescribable wonders. 'They could be argent-powered,' I said slowly. 'Some of those things they sell. Certainly some of the things they use. If it was hidden, how would anybody know? And if nobody knew, how would anyone compete?'

'They do have remarkably potent charms,' Jay agreed. 'And a long history of unusually powerful magicians.'

My eyes grew big. 'Forget your earlier conspiracy theory, Jay. *This* is the real stuff!'

14

'I FEEL WE NEED confirmation,' I said.

Val nodded. 'We are running too much on speculation. I'd like evidence.'

'House thought Crystobel was telling the truth,' I said. Which wasn't evidence, but we all trusted house.

'I do not doubt House's instincts,' Val said. 'Or whatever they are. But what did Crystobel actually say?'

'She said that *little* has survived from Cicily's life,' I said. 'Define "little".'

Val nodded. '"Little" could still include the books we're hoping for.'

'And regarding Cicily's work, um,' I thought back. 'She said Cicily's work was unrealised at the time of her death — which I took to mean nothing ever came of it at all. But perhaps it was completed *after* her death.'

'By her son,' Val agreed. 'For example.' Her hands were moving; she was stroking the arms of her new chair. Was there *argent* built into its frame? Was that why its levitation charms were so much better than either Val or I could manage?

'Still isn't evidence,' I sighed.

'We need something concrete,' Val agreed.

'She *said* argent couldn't be manufactured—' I said.

'No,' said Val. 'She said there was nothing in *alchemy* that would do it. That is not the same thing at all.'

'Giddy gods. You mean we might have been on the wrong track since the beginning?' Why was I even surprised? We'd never found any proof of anybody's making any form of alchemy work, ever.

'*Would* that even be unusual?' said Val.

She had a point.

'If only we had something more... material,' I mused.

'I've always preferred paper to hot air,' Val agreed.

When Jay realised both of us were looking at him, he visibly balked. As in, he took a whole step back, and raised his hands. 'Hey. There's only so far alumni status will get me.'

'And how far is that?' I asked.

'Um.'

'How about sending in a bulk request for anything attributed to Cicily Werewode-Elvyng?'

'Surely they would never allow it.'

'That's sort of the point.'

Jay blinked. 'Oh. Right.'

Val opened up her laptop, and turned it about to face Jay. 'Here. Use this.'

As Jay clicked and typed, I thought. Our suspicions were huge, bordering upon crazy. But the more I thought about it, the more sense it made. 'Crystobel Elvyng,' I said aloud. 'Why did she really come here?'

Val directed a narrow-eyed look at the wall, deep in thought, but said nothing.

'I mean, if there was really nothing for us to find, she could have just had her secretary phone you, or send an email. Why bother coming all this way in person?' I had to kick myself for not having thought of that before.

Now I was thinking differently. Why had she come here, if not to discourage us from digging any further into her family's most lucrative secrets?

'It still isn't evidence,' said Val.

No. We couldn't take a conspiracy theory to Milady and expect to be taken seriously. And Milady couldn't take a bundle of suppositions, surmises and suspicions to the Elvyngs and expect to be taken seriously.

Hell, at this point we had nothing. Real evidence that Cicily Werewode, or her descendants, succeeded at creating the magickal silver, by alchemy or any other art? No.

Evidence that she'd ever written down, or shared those processes if she had? No again. Proof that the Elvyngs had inherited her legacy? Well, only the will — and it made no reference to what Godfrey Elvyng's inheritance had consisted of.

I suffered a moment's gnawing, gut-dropping panic when I realised we could be wrong on all points. Cicily might have dabbled in alchemy as a very young woman, and stopped. The Elvyngs might be protecting quite different secrets. We could be chasing nothing but wishes and dreams.

But there were too many small links and subtle clues to really believe that. Cicily's possession of Mary Werewode's work, for one, and Mary had been a known enthusiast for strange arts such as alchemy. Cicily's Yllanfalen grandfather, for another, and the fact that he'd come from the very same town that once boasted the Moonsilver Mines.

Valentine *Argent*ein, and the discovery that *argent* not only meant "silver" but specifically magickal silver, at least in some circles. And somehow, Crystobel Elvyng had known this. We hadn't come across the term *argent* anywhere else.

I rubbed my temples, frustrated. So many hints, so many maybes. Enough to keep us digging; not enough to give us any real answers.

'If only we could talk to Cicily,' I sighed.

'Her ghost?' Val raised both eyebrows at me. 'You've been spending way too much time with Zareen.'

'Or, not enough. I wish she was here.' Not solely for the purposes of the mission. I'd been missing Zar. Watching her break had been hard; I couldn't begin to imagine what life was like inside her head, with the powers she possessed. She'd always seemed untouchable before. A powerhouse of a woman, always full of energy, and a brightness I now realised had sometimes been forced. Brittle.

'Not every ghost can be fished up out of history,' Val said. 'Most of them go quietly on to wherever they're supposed to go.'

True. The kind we had been hobnobbing with lately had been… different. Bound, mostly, to the houses they'd lived in — or been taken to. Some of them through their own will, some of them trapped there.

I dashed off a quick text to Zar (*Hey scary lady, how's the holiday?*), even as my mind wandered back to the portrait of Cicily Werewode. Something about it teased at me, kept returning to my mind. Maybe it was the faint note of melancholy inherent in her expression, or the sadness of her exile in a tiny garret room of her own house. Why had they stashed her up there? Especially if our suspicions were correct: that would make Cicily Werewode the most important figure in Elvyng history.

With which idea, I'd answered my own question. If they couldn't or wouldn't share Cicily's (possible) achievements with the world, they couldn't prominently celebrate her connection with their family, either.

'Denied,' said Jay, looking up from Val's laptop.

I went around the desk and bent over his shoulder. *The Elvyng Archives are unable to satisfy your request.* Apologies, etc.

'What does that mean?' I said. 'Could that mean they're already checked out, or something?'

Jay shook his head. 'If that's the case they put you on a wait list, and send an estimate of how long you'll have to wait to get the books. And if they don't have anything on the subject you're interested in, or the document's been lost, they'll say something like *We have not been able to match your request to any extant resources in our archive.* This, I haven't seen before.'

I straightened up, pleased but also frustrated. Yes, this stonewalling was suggestive. They didn't want anyone poking too far into Cicily's business. Asking for her will was one thing, considering how little telling information it contained. Asking for all her private papers was another.

'How did her journal end up in York?' I said, struck suddenly by the thought. 'Why isn't that also buried in the Elvyng Archives?'

Val frowned in thought, and tapped her favourite pen against her lips. 'It dates from before her marriage,' she said. 'So in theory, the Elvyngs have no real right to claim it.'

Jay said, 'But she must have given it away before her death, or it would have gone to her son with the rest of her personal things. And thence into the Academy Archives.'

'So who did she give it to?' I said. 'And why?'

'And how did it end up in York,' Val echoed, retrieving her laptop from Jay. 'I'm going to send a query about its provenance. They might be able to tell us who donated it to their library.'

We were back to the question of Cicily's relatives again, and I simply couldn't stand it.

'No,' I said.

Val looked up. 'No? No what?'

'No to everything! I am *done* with running in circles after Cicily's non-existent paper trail. If there's anything there to be discovered at all, the Elvyngs will stonewall us forever, and anything Cicily might have given to some other relative is untraceable. The whole thing is hopeless and we're wasting our time.'

Val stopped typing. 'I don't disagree, but it's what we've got. Do you have a better idea?'

'I have a *different* idea,' I said. 'Forget Cicily's obscure familial connections, and forget the Elvyngs. Let them keep their secrets, if they must. Why don't we just ask Cicily herself?'

Jay and Val stared at me.

'Um,' said Jay. 'Are we back to that thing about Zareen and Cicily's ghost? Because it's a crazy long shot there's even a ghost left to talk to—'

'It isn't about that,' I said.

Val sat back, folded her arms, and gave me the narrow-eyed look. 'I believe I see a Patented Vesper-Classic Crazy Plan aloft on the horizon.'

'Coming in fast,' I agreed, beaming. 'Wanna hear it?'

'Do we have a choice?' muttered Jay.

'Nope,' I said. 'Listen, there's something I haven't told you.' I held up both my hands, and wiggled my fingers. 'There are one or two, er, lingering effects going on with me after that whole Vales of Wonder thing—'

'Is this about those zappy little spurts of magick?' said Val.

'How did you know about those?'

'Five days ago you left a scorch mark on the cover of *The Life and Work of The Great Alchemist Nicolas Flamel.*'

'I *did*?' I gasped. 'And you didn't have me cleaning the latrines in penance?'

Val tilted her head. 'It isn't a great book.'

'Well. Those zappy little spurts can be useful, for all that they're involuntary. When I was at the Academy I touched the portrait of Cicily Werewode—'

'*What*?' snapped Jay.

'Only a tiny bit! I didn't harm it, I swear.'

Jay rolled his eyes, but mercifully said no more.

'Anyway, my fingers did that fizzy thing, but instead of scorching the painting — thankfully — it, um, cleaned it.'

'Cleaned...?' said Jay, his brows shooting up.

I nodded emphatically. 'Cleaned off all the centuries of dirt until it looked new-painted. And there was a sheen of moonlight in her hair, and — and something else. I hardly know. Only I haven't been able to stop thinking about the painting ever since. Something in her eyes nags at me. It's like she was looking right at me, trying to tell me something.'

'That's extremely interesting,' said Jay, and while I thought I heard a shade of sarcasm about the words, he did look impressed. At least, that's how I chose to interpret that intent, searching look he directed at me. 'How exactly does it help us?'

'Jay, I can't say how, but... what if she *was* trying to communicate with me? That painting isn't normal. I have no idea how, but I believe some part of Cicily Werewode lingers there, and why would she if she didn't have something to *do*?'

'Her ghost, again? In a painting?'

I shook my head. 'No. Well… probably not. I don't know, Jay. I just have a… hunch.'

He grinned. 'Like a Milady-in-training.'

'I can only hope to be that awesome someday, though by preference I'd like to hang on to my corporeal form.'

He gave a tiny sigh. 'So. Let's see if I'm getting the hang of the Ves Crazy Plan. You think that portrait will somehow answer all the lingering questions we've run into about Cicily Werewode, the work she did, and where it went.'

'Right!'

'And you'd like to test this by…' he paused in thought, looking me up and down as though he might see signs of my intentions emblazoned upon my dress. 'Submitting an official, formal request to borrow the painting, via official, formal channels? No. That would be far too obvious, and besides it would—'

'Take *ages*,' I said. 'Val, you remember the debacle of the Greendale journals?'

Val put her face in her hands, and groaned. 'Four months. *Four.* Every single conceivable run-around…'

I nodded. 'We don't have weeks or months to spend jumping through the interminable hoops they call bureaucracy. You see that, Jay, don't you?'

'I do,' he allowed, inclining his head. 'And while I hate to admit it, the chances of such a request being approved are pretty slim, especially now that Crystobel Elvyng's made it her business to try to stall us.'

'Exactly!'

'So there is nothing to be done but to sneak in and mess with their painting without their knowledge.'

'It's for the good of magick,' I said gravely. 'If we can pull this off, the Elvyngs won't need to rely on magickal silver or argent or whatever anymore. There'll be plenty of magick, for everything.'

'Supposing that they *are* relying on argent,' said Jay, with annoying but perfectly correct pedantry. 'And then their business will collapse, because the very best of their wares today will become the very least we can do in the future.'

I waved this away. 'They'll adapt, and make even more amazing stuff.'

Jay checked the time. 'Right. If we leave now, we can have this next exciting, law-defying adventure over by teatime.'

'Well...' I said.

Jay looked at me. 'There's more? Say there isn't more.'

'Um, I think we have to do it at night.'

15

'At night,' he repeated.

'Remember the glimmer-of-moonlight thing I mentioned? And Mary Werewode and her moon-bathing and moonsilver and *all* of that. Giddy gods know why, but there *is* a pattern there — you said so yourself, Jay! — and I'm really curious to know what might happen if I "mess with" her painting when the moon's up.'

'The Elvyng Academy is not open at night,' said Jay.

'I know that.'

'So that makes it a case of actual breaking and entering.'

'I know.'

'Which is an actual crime.'

'Not if you aren't stealing anything.'

'I'm... pretty sure it's still a crime, Ves, even if you aren't a burglar.'

'It'll only be for a few minutes.'

'Right, because it's the *duration* that determines the severity of the offence.'

I looked, rather pleadingly, at Val.

She watched our back-and-forth with a small smile. 'I don't know,' she said when she caught my eye, and shook her head. 'Watching you try to justify yourself to, of all people, Jay? I'm liking it.'

'Hey,' said Jay. 'Of all people?'

Val could hardly explain that Jay was both new and supposedly my responsibility, or had been for most of his time with the Society so far. Superiors I'd withstood without blinking; I'd even circumvented Milady's orders on occasion, if I felt a deep enough need to do so. I'd never worked so hard to gain anyone's approval as I did Jay's. Don't ask me why; I don't understand it myself.

Maybe I am just wicked, and his very strait-laced nature operates upon me like the proverbial red flag to a bull.

Maybe it's the simple fact that he is usually right, and this irks me because I am evil.

I rushed on. 'If we do it tonight, we could have answers by the morning—'

'*We?*' said Jay, with that ominous, shadowy frown he has when he's really unhappy about something. I could practically hear thunder rumbling in the distance.

'Okay, me,' I said quickly. 'I'll go alone, if you'll just help me get there and back.'

'No.'

'You can wait outside.'

'No. Ves, I don't—' He stopped, and actually rubbed his temples in frustration. 'Ves, remarkable as you are, I have no idea how you haven't ended up in prison yet.'

I scoffed at this. 'I don't make a *habit* of breaking and entering.'

'*Once would be enough.*'

'Only if you get caught?'

'Which, of course, you never could.'

'Jay. Look. I hear you, and you're right, but do you have a better idea? Because we've been following the library trail for weeks on end, and all we've got to show for it is a tangled mess of dead-end clues.'

Jay looked, apparently for confirmation, at Val, who spread her hands in an I-can't-help-you gesture. 'More or less the case,' she said. 'There might be a breakthrough ahead, but...'

'There also might not,' I finished. 'At this point, I would put money on not.'

Val nodded. 'I hate to say it, but if Ves is in any way right about that painting, it should be explored.'

I beamed triumphantly at Jay.

But he shook his head. 'I don't actually dispute that. But breaking into other people's houses, at night or at any other time, is not okay, no matter the motive.'

'I—' I began.

'*Nor is it wise,*' he said severely, frowning at me.

'So about that better idea?' I said.

To my infinite surprise and delight, he said: 'I do, actually, have a better idea.'

A FEW HOURS LATER saw us on Elvyng property once more. *Not* breaking and entering.

'You know, if I'd realised you still had slumber party privileges at the Academy we could have skipped the entire breaking-and-entering conversation,' I said as we approached the main doors (Jay having walked me quickly, quickly past the Emporium).

'It's not the sort of thing one happens to mention,' Jay answered, and rang the bell.

As though anything with the Elvyngs is merely ordinary. The bell, in this instance, was represented by a small, oval panel of magick-charged gem set innocuously into the great stone frame. Labradorite, by the looks of it: pallid but glimmering with colours. I hadn't noticed it before, because when I had arrived earlier with Val, the doors had been open to the public.

All Jay had to do was wave a palm in front of the panel. A glitter of magick rippled over its surface, and — I kid you not — an actual, socking enormous bell *tolled* from somewhere within. I judge its size from the depth and resonance of the bell's tone: it sounded like the kind that usually crowns the tops of cathedral spires.

'I bet that's popular in the middle of the night,' I commented, wide-eyed.

'People don't usually ring the bell in the middle of the night,' Jay pointed out. Quite rightly, considering that he added, 'Anyone trying to visit at 3am is either in possession of a key, or is here to rob the place.'

I blushed, for without Jay's surprise sleepover credentials that's exactly what I would have done. Well, not the robbing part. Just the sneaking in without an invitation part.

We did not have to wait long. Soon after the last, echoing sounds of the great bell died away, the heavy oak door unlatched, and swung slowly open. I peeked inside, expecting to see somebody effecting this opening, but I saw no one.

Like I said, nothing about Elvyng could be ordinary.

Jay sauntered in at his ease, and wasted no time looking around for a welcoming party. The doors slid smoothly shut behind us — audibly locking and bolting themselves, to my mild consternation — and I followed as Jay walked straight through the hall, down a corridor, up a flight of stairs and knocked at a door at the top. Zero hesitation. He knew the place like the back of his hand.

'Come in,' called someone within.

The voice — quite low for a female, and smooth — proved to belong to a woman of about Jay's age, or maybe a year or two younger. We'd found the music room: small though the chamber was, space had somehow been found for a gloriously shiny grand piano, a row of guitars, two violins and a collection of bright, silvery pipes that immediately drew my eye. I didn't see anything quite like my own syrinx set, but one or two were close.

Jay's academy contact sat at a desk in the corner, its surface covered in sheet music and notepaper. She looked up as we came in, grinned at Jay, and eyed me with frank curiosity. She had sleek, black hair worn loose, skin a couple of shades lighter than Jay's, and fabulous brown eyes almost amber in colour. 'Jay,' she said, her gaze flicking again to me. 'It's been a while.'

'Been busy,' he murmured, smiling back. 'You know how that goes.'

'Still incapable of taking a day off?'

'Like you were ever any better.'

'Family curse.' The lady grinned.

'I prefer "trait",' Jay retorted. 'Er, this is Cordelia Vesper, my associate at the Society. Ves, this is my sister Rina. She's a music professor at the Academy.'

I looked at Rina with fresh interest. She looked to be in her late twenties, which probably made her the sibling closest to him in age.

Rina came over to me and shook my hand. I didn't miss the enquiring look she directed at Jay as she stepped back. Was she silently asking as to the purport of our mission, or was she silently enquiring about me?

Smoothly, Jay let it pass. 'Thanks for letting us in,' he said.

She nodded, watching his face, but being Jay he was impassive. 'I've had a room fixed up for you, though why you want to be in the attic is beyond me. I don't think anyone cleans up there more than once in a blue moon.'

She was fishing for details, so that meant Jay hadn't really told her anything. Interesting. 'We appreciate it,' I told her. 'It's a great help.'

Rina nodded, plainly mystified, but too polite to push for details. 'You didn't want your old dorm?' she said to Jay, with a trace of a smile.

'I imagined it otherwise occupied by now.'

'Was, but it hasn't yet been reassigned for the upcoming year. It'll be empty, if you want to take a look.'

'That's fine.' Jay shook his head. 'We'll let you get back to your work, and go get started.'

'Started?' she echoed, looking from Jay to me.

Jay waved this off, already making for the door. I hesitated, for surely she deserved *some* kind of an inkling as to what we were doing? But I vaguely realised I had strayed into Sibling Rivalry territory, an area I was hopelessly ill-equipped to cope with, and decided to leave well alone.

'Aren't you going to tell her anything?' I said once we were fairly out of earshot.

'About what?' he said, without slowing down.

'About what we're doing here?' I prodded.

'Nope.'

'Come on. She's doing us a huge favour.'

'How is that relevant?'

'*Jay.* What *did* you tell her?'

'I said I was in the area, looking for somewhere to stay, and wanted to... revisit old haunts.'

Whether or not a music professor was allowed to invite friends to stay overnight, I didn't choose to speculate. If she was bending the rules, she seemed happy to do so.

'How obliging of her to swallow such a transparent story.'

'She'll get her revenge at some point.'

'And what am I supposed to be doing?'

'Er.'

'I hope you didn't let her think I'd be spending the night here with you.'

'The idea that an attractive, intelligent woman might want to spend the night with me wouldn't enter her head,' he said, stopping at the top of what I hoped was the final flight of stairs. 'Nor yours, apparently.'

'I--' I began.

'Which way did you go from here?'

I swallowed my objections. Stop digging, Ves. 'I think it was this way.' I turned left, towards a dusty and faded velvet-clad chair that looked vaguely familiar. 'Aha!' I crowed, elated, for there was a door I definitely knew, and when I pushed it open, there was the tiny garret I recalled. Still dusty and smelling of mildew. And there on the wall was—

An empty space, the picture hook still protruding from the wall.

'It's gone,' I gasped.

16

'CRYSTOBEL ELVYNG,' I HISSED. 'She's been here.'

Jay held up his hands. 'Hang on. Maybe there's another explanation.'

'If so, that would have to be a *huge* coincidence.'

'Coincidences do happen. That's why there's a word for it.'

'All right.'

'And why would Crystobel take it away?'

'She knows I was up here, and didn't want us to examine it further.'

'How would she know that?'

I opened my mouth, and paused. 'Um. Someone saw me?'

Jay shrugged. 'Or it has nothing to do with Crystobel.'

'Why would people randomly move paintings around?'

'Not at random. I can't say I paid much attention to the relative positions of the Academy's paintings in my day, but there are rather a lot of them. And they're sensitive to light damage, as you well know. The more prominent positions also tend to be well-lit, and no painting can be safely left in strong light for long.'

'I still think it's a huge coincidence.'

'Take heart. I might be proved wrong, and you can hare after the perfidious Crystobel after all, Wand raised to destroy.'

I didn't miss his use of the singular pronoun. This was one wild escapade I'd be going on alone. 'So,' I said. 'Where do you suppose it might have been taken to?'

'Somewhere more prominent,' said Jay, turning on his heel as he spoke, and marching out of the garret again. Back down the stairs we went, down and down — and found the portrait, inevitably, in the main hallway, right over the fireplace.

'We walked straight past it,' I said, tasting bitter chagrin. 'What's worse, it might even be our fault that it's been moved down here. Val was asking the tour guide about Cicily, and she was the one who told us about the portrait. They're probably responding to visitor interest.'

'I'll get you a hair shirt to wear when we get back,' Jay promised. 'In the meantime: what was it you were planning to do with it?'

We stood in front of the fireplace in the darkened hall, both of us staring dumbly up at Cicily's face. We hadn't wanted to advertise our presence by switching on lights, and Cicily looked eerier than ever in the faint, harsh glow emitted by our phone screens. She'd seemed welcoming before, but now…

I shrugged off the thought. 'We need to take her outside,' I said, and before Jay could (wisely) stop me, I'd reached up and plucked the portrait off the wall.

I paused for a breathless second, just in case some kind of magickal alarm sounded and brought a vengeful Rina Patel bursting in upon us (not to mention my new favourite nemesis, Crystobel).

When nothing happened, I turned triumphantly to the front door. 'Open, please,' I said, either to Jay or to the door, whichever felt disposed to answer.

As it happens, it was the door. Jay moved to open it for me, but already it was in creaking motion, and moonlight came streaming in.

Once outside, I stood looking up at the serene heavens. It was just about fully dark, and the clear skies were bathed in moonglow. 'It would be a bit more perfect were it full moon,' I said. 'But three-quarters ought to do.' Carefully, carefully — *do not drop it, Cordelia Vesper, or there will never be enough hair-shirts in the world for you* — I turned the painting face up to the moonlight, wrapping all ten fingers around the frame. 'Come on,' I muttered. 'Time to fizz.'

'Fizz?' said Jay, watching over my shoulder.

'Those jazzy little sparks Val spoke of. Now's the time.' I shook the painting a little, rubbed the frame with my fingers (it worked for Aladdin's lamp, why not a sixteenth century painting?), and even hummed a couple of bars of *Syllphyllan*.

To no avail. Not so much as a flicker of a response did Cicily give, and the moonlight was gone from her hair.

Jay looked around. 'I hate to rush you, but if we're caught standing out here with an irreplaceable painting, I don't know who is going to believe we weren't trying to steal it.'

'It's okay,' I said absently. 'Rina will save you.'

Jay snorted. 'We'd more likely get her fired.'

I searched Cicily's face for clues, and stared into her limpid blue eyes. 'Come on,' I whispered. 'You had something to say, I know it. Speak to me.'

She didn't. But something else happened. It began as a spark in the depths of those eyes, distant as a star, so faint I held my breath for fear of scaring it away again. The glimmer grew, and spread, until her eyes were bright with life and — I could swear — comprehension. Recognition.

'Ves,' Jay breathed in awe. 'You appear to be onto something.'

'Thank you, doubting Thomas.' I whispered the words, still unwilling to risk disrupting whatever delicate process was underway. A faint blush of health returned to her oil-painted cheeks, a sheen of something no artist, however talented, could ever capture: life itself. A soft night-breeze ruffled my hair, and Cicily's also stirred in the wind.

'This is not a ghost,' Jay said.

'No,' I agreed. 'She's far too alive.'

And she was, yet also still a construct of canvas and oils. My fingers were fizzing in earnest by then, and I couldn't have said whether that, too, was a coincidence, or whether the wayward magick in me responded to some peculiar property of the painting. Either way, Cicily Werewode's beautiful Yllanfalen eyes blinked once, twice; and then she spoke.

'Who...?' she whispered, her voice distant and echoing, as though she spoke from very far away.

Then she said, 'Mary? Is that you?'

I swallowed. 'It— it is not Mary. It's—'

'Grandfather?' said Cicily.

Did she hear me at all?

'Why's she trying to talk to Mary?' Jay hissed in my ear. 'Mary Werewode died long before she was born.'

A fair question. 'Maybe a different Mary,' I suggested. 'It's been a common name since approximately forever.'

'Coincidence? Again?'

I knew he was teasing me, but I wavered. And caved. 'No. You're right. That's too many coincidences. It *has* to be the same Mary.'

'There's no other possible explanation,' Jay agreed, and I heard the grin in his words.

Ignoring Jay, I touched a forefinger to the painting's surface, although not right over Cicily's face. 'Cicily,' I said. 'Can you hear me?'

Her strange, animated face blinked again, her mouth an 'O' of dismay. Her eyes moved, narrowed, as though she were trying to see out of the painting. 'Mary?' she said again.

'It is not Mary. I am... Cordelia.' "Ves" would not sound like a name to her, and I didn't want to add to her confusion.

'Cor...' she whispered, faintly, as though drawing farther off.

'Cordelia! Yes!' I was gripping the painting's frame too hard in my excitement; I forced myself to relax, until the white faded from my knuckles. It wouldn't do to rend the thing to bits out of sheer enthusiasm.

'I do not know any Cordelia.' The words barely reached my ears, so soft-spoken they were. Her eyes drifted shut, opened, shut again.

'Wait,' I said, panicked. 'All right, it's Mary. Mary Werewode.'

The eyes opened once more, and looked directly at me. Sharp. Keen. I quailed a little, caught out in a puerile lie — but she was still awake.

'You are different,' she said.

'Many years have passed.'

'How many?' Moonlight rode a wave of her hair, vanishing with a glitter.

'Over four hundred years.'

Cicily fell silent, probably with astonishment.

Jay, however, spoke. 'Ves,' he said, in a low, urgent tone which took *me* by surprise. 'This is not good magick.'

'*Good* magick? There is no such thing as good or bad magick, Jay. Zareen should have been enough to teach you that.'

He shook his head. 'Then call it *unobjectionable* and *questionable* magick, if you will, and this is deeply questionable.'

'Why?' I kept a close eye on Cicily, unsure whether she followed or cared for our conversation. She gave no sign of doing either.

'I've... heard of this.'

'This?' I gave the painting a tiny, illustrative shake.

'Yes. It's a kind of— of trap. It isn't a ghost, not exactly, and she's not bound to the painting in the same way that Millie's bound into the walls of her farmhouse. It's similar, but not—'

'Jay, spit it out. Please.'

'It's done while the subject is still alive.'

'What.'

'Or it was. I need hardly add that it's completely, totally banned now, even on a voluntary subject.'

'*Voluntary?*'

'Some people sought the procedure. After all, if your living essence is bound into a very long-lived item like a painting, then you don't die.'

I stared at the semblance of Cicily Werewode, my skin crawling at the idea. She hadn't died. Not because she or her ancestors had discovered the mythical elixir of immortality, but because she'd resigned her living, breathing personhood in favour of the cramped confines of a painting about six inches across.

Willingly? Or not?

'Cicily,' I said grimly. 'Cicily Werewode. How did this portrait come to exist?'

No answer. Was this the first time in centuries that Cicily, such as she was, had spoken? Long stupor had made her vague, sleepy.

I swallowed. 'She looks so young.'

'Doesn't necessarily mean she was young when this was done to her. A person's living essence has little to do with the age of their physical shell, after all, and the artist could paint her any way she liked.'

'Is she... is she a whole person, in there? Or more like — like an echo?'

Jay shrugged. 'My knowledge is limited. I can't answer that.'

'Why haven't *I* ever heard of it?'

A pause. Possibly an embarrassed pause. 'I shouldn't have, either,' Jay admitted. 'It's not only banned, all books on the subject are banned from circulation, too. They tend to be under lock and key... I'd forgotten all about it until just now.'

A lock and key which had served as little bar to a younger, very curious Jay, I surmised. The (questionable) fruits of attending so prestigious an academy — or had he gone delving in the archives of the Hidden University? Despite myself, I was a little bit impressed. I'd never have thought that strait-laced Jay's thirst for knowledge might have ever overpowered his caution.

Then again, where had that extreme caution come from? Perhaps he'd been caught, sometime in the past. Perhaps he'd had good reason to swear off similar transgressions for the future.

I filed the thought away. Now wasn't the time for pestering for details.

'This is creepy as hell,' I muttered. 'Seriously, I thought hanging around with Zareen was the creepiest my life was ever going to get.'

'It ought to be. I'd really like to think nobody's done this in at least a couple of centuries.'

But was it wrong, when performed for a willing subject? Everyone ought to have the right to make such a choice, surely.

I remembered the trace of melancholy I thought I'd seen in Cicily's face, and I wondered.

'Right,' I said, giving myself a mental shake. 'We're getting side-tracked. We'll have to report this to Milady; I don't know if something needs to be done here.'

'Bet you anything you like there's a similar portrait of Mary Werewode out there somewhere,' said Jay.

'*Yes*,' I hissed. 'Not a book, but a Mary-painting. That's why she's trying to talk to Mary.'

'I am now just a little gutted over how many hours we've spent searching for written records.'

'We? *I've* spent three weeks looking for books that never existed. You've been on the job for about thirty-six hours.'

'Have I ever mentioned how deeply I admire your dedication?' said Jay.

'If I thought you meant it, I'd be flattered.'

'Maybe I do.'

'Still getting side tracked,' I said. 'We're here about argent, not paintings.'

'Or flattery. My bad.'

Something happened when I said that word, *argent.* One of my fizzes, to say the least: magick sparked in a rush, so potent I feared I'd set the frame on fire. Magick and moonlight rippled over the canvas's surface, briefly obscuring Cicily's face in a haze of pale silver.

Sudden enlightenment dawned. I turned the painting over, and saw nothing on the back but a plain wooden backing. Nonetheless, I knew without doubt. 'This thing is painted on argent,' I whispered. 'The frame is probably full of the stuff, too.'

'I bet argent would make the entire person-preserving process a lot easier,' said Jay grimly. 'Maybe the Elvyngs aren't wrong to keep a lid on it.'

I doubted that had much to do with their motive, but what did I know? Perhaps they were acting out of a sense of civic responsibility as much as out of greed. People were complex.

Anyway. 'Cicily Werewode-Elvyng,' I said, more loudly. 'Did you discover the secret of argent?'

The soft lights had faded by then, leaving her image clear once more. She looked enlivened, her eyes brighter, her cheeks flushed with a glow of healthful colour. The effects of moonlight? Magick? Argent? Some combination of all three?

'I did not,' she said, distant still, but more clearly.

My heart sank a little. Crystobel Elvyng had indeed been telling the truth.

Jay spoke up. 'What about your son?'

Cicily's head shook, side to side, in a gentle negative.

That surprised me — and dismayed me. What, had Crystobel been right about everything?

'Why not?' said Jay.

Her brow creased in mild puzzlement. 'What need had we?' said she. ''Twas your own work, Mary. Why do you now ask this of me?'

'*Mary*—?' I said, thunderstruck. *Mary* had discovered it, all the way back in the thirteen hundreds? Crazy, moon-bathing Mary? No wonder we'd struck out on finding further accounts of Cicily's work. Having penned her early journals, she'd stopped investigating after all — *not* because she got married, but because she realised her great-great-great-grandmother had already succeeded. And her husband's family had benefited spectacularly from the find.

But how had that secret been kept from everyone else? Had Mary's reputation for eccentricity been enough?

'Now for the billion-pound question,' I muttered under my breath. 'Cicily, I have lost my work. The years have stolen it away. Where is it, my beloved great-granddaughter? I would have it restored to me.'

Cicily, to my extreme surprise, laughed. Naturally she had a high, tinkling laugh, sweet like a soft summer breeze. For heaven's sake. 'Have you, then, forgot?'

'Yes. I am seven hundred years old, and very forgetful.'

'Then you must go back to the source, must not you?'

'The source?' This received no response, and to my alarm the vagueness was creeping back into Cicily's eyes. I received the chilling impression that not quite a whole person lingered here, if ever she had been. Time had cracked and weathered her, and what was left was but a fraction of her former self.

'Cicily,' I said urgently. 'Where is the source? I have forgotten that, too.'

The brow creased again, gently. 'Argentein?' she said.

My heart thrilled. Argentein! A link with the mysterious Valentine! 'Who is—' I began, and stopped.

Jay realised it the same moment I did. 'Valentine Argentein,' he gasped. 'It isn't a person. It's a place.'

'Giddy sodding gods.'

17

I didn't bother texting Val this time. I called her. If that meant dragging her out of the library and whichever book she was absorbed in, so be it.

'Yes?' she said, after three rings. The word had a dangerous edge to it.

'Valentine Argentein,' I said.

'Ves! You found him?'

'Val, you are not going to believe this.'

While Jay nipped back into the academy to return the painting — my having reluctantly let it go — I rushed through an only slightly garbled account of everything we had just experienced.

'Slow down,' said Val more than once, and I tried, but my heart was galloping and my fingers were zapping with magick and I was fit to burst with excitement.

'She's a painting,' Val said at one point. 'A painting? *She*, Cicily Werewode, is a painting? Ves, have you gone off your rocker?'

And later, 'You pretended to be Mary Werewode and she bought it? Has *she* gone off her rocker?'

At length we got around to: 'Valentine Argentein is a gods-damned *place.* That makes so much sense you have no idea.'

'It... does?'

'It was driving me crazy, this supposed author that vanished into thin air. But I was wrong to interpret the name as the author, not the title. The book has the air of a personal journal about it, that's the thing. It's hand-written, and so is what *now* turns out to be the title, but I previously interpreted as the name of the writer. As a work it's informally arranged, only loosely coherent, and pretty impenetrable. And I now have no earthly idea who penned it, but maybe that doesn't matter. The only problem is...' I heard a rustling of papers, and otherwise silence for a while. 'I don't think there's any real mention of Valentine Argentein in the book, excepting the title. So if the book isn't really about this place Argentein, what's it for?'

'What else is in it, besides that one bit about *magycke silver* or whatever it was?'

'A whole lot of confused ramblings. I wonder...' Silence, and more rustling.

I ventured upon a tentative point of my own. 'Is this maybe what the Lorekeeper was talking about? Some kind of code?'

'Could be. Could be. It doesn't make a lot of sense as it is, certainly, and it's hard to imagine why anyone would bother writing down such gibberish if it doesn't mean anything.'

'Get Cicily's journal back from the cryptographers. There's nothing to find there.'

'And give 'em this. Right. Begs the question, though: where's this mysterious source of Mary Werewode's work?'

'I got the impression it's in Argentein.'

'She didn't give you any clues as to where that is?'

'Not really. She's a faded excuse for a person, kept blanking on us. And while I'd love to take the portrait with us and keep pumping her for information, we can't exactly abscond with it.'

'No,' Val sighed. 'I suppose you can't.'

Her dejection echoed my own. 'I have two ideas.'

'Tell me.'

'One, she seemed to think she could talk to Mary Werewode, who of course must have died long before she was born. Unless she didn't. We think there must be a chatty portrait of Mary somewhere about, and Cicily must have got hold of it.'

'Right. Where's the portrait?'

'No clue.'

'Excellent. Idea number two?'

I hesitated. 'I'm speculating,' I cautioned.

'What else is new.'

'Fair. Look, Cicily mentioned her grandfather. She thought she might be talking to him, too.'

'Her grandfather, the Yllanfalen?'

'Right. The one that came from Everynden, where the Moonsilver Mines were.'

A pause. 'You think Argentein might refer to those mines?'

'Total guess,' I said. 'But yes. Yes, I do.'

'But they were emptied by Cicily's time, no?'

'Exactly.'

'Not following.'

'Cicily mentioned the "source", with a weird emphasis, like it should mean something to Mary. Well, the mines were the age-old source of moonsilver, or argent. What better place to put your secret moonsilver lab than an abandoned mineshaft that was once bristling with the stuff? Maybe there are traces of it still there. Maybe there's an atmosphere, a memory — something. I don't know, I may be talking rubbish, but it...'

'Makes a weird kind of sense,' Val finished. 'I've another thought.'

'Hit me with it.'

'What if…' she hesitated. 'We have no idea what process they might have gone through to produce their *argent*, right? Except that Crystobel thinks it wasn't alchemy.'

'Right.'

'Nothing in Cicily's journal. Nothing in any of Mary's letters that might hint at it, even allowing for deliberate obfuscation and bizarre code. In other words, we have no evidence that *such a process exists.*'

It was my turn to say, 'Not following.'

'Maybe it doesn't exist. Crystobel told the truth. You can't manufacture argent.'

'But Cicily said—'

'Cicily didn't deny the existence of a source of argent. That doesn't mean it has anything to do with alchemy.'

'She— I did ask her if she'd discovered the secret of argent, or if her son had, and she said no. That there was no need, because it was Mary's own work…'

'But she never said there was an alchemical secret?'

'She… no, she didn't.'

'Maybe because there wasn't. Whatever they did, it wasn't alchemy, or not in the way we've been thinking. They weren't reciting mumbo-jumbo over blocks of silver, or immersing them in chemical solutions. They weren't waving magick wands over them or drowning them in charms. They weren't transmuting anything, in short.' Val was talking faster and faster, working herself up to one of her genius crescendos. 'Ves, what if you're right?'

'I like being right,' I said — doubtfully, being still far behind wherever Val's scintillating intellect had taken her. 'What am I right about this time?'

'The mines. Maybe they weren't transmuting some base substance into argent. Maybe they found a way to — to restart the mines.'

'Restart the—' I stopped, because she was right. I'd spoken just a moment ago about a lingering atmosphere, or a memory. Entrenched magick. An entire network of mineshafts bristling with argent must have held an entire ocean of magick, so to speak, before we'd finally chipped away the last block. But what of the rock that remained? What if it *could* be... encouraged? Enchanted?

'Moon-bathing,' I said, apropos of nothing. 'The portrait activated under moonlight, with a bit of magickal fizz to help it along.'

'Okay. Maybe Mary's moon-bathing wasn't about restoring her own youth. Maybe she was talking about the mines.'

'We need to go there.'

'At night.'

'Right.'

'Ves, one thing though.' More rustling. 'The Elvyngs. If they *know* about this, then anything you find down there is likely to be under their control.'

'Got it.'

'You realise what that means?'

'Opposition.'

'To say the least. They won't welcome anyone's snooping. It's a literally priceless secret.'

I paused, and thought. My instinct was, as always, to barrel in and look around and figure out the details once we got there. But Val had a point. Jay would be dead set against such foolhardiness, and for once I knew he'd be right without having to be talked into it. So then, what? How to proceed?

'I think it's time to pass the buck,' I decided.

'Mm. Get back here. I'll see if I can rouse Milady.'

'Milady sleeps?' The idea, for some reason, astonished me. Maybe because one doesn't picture a disembodied voice having physical needs like the rest of us.

'Who knows?' Upon which enlightening comment, Val hung up the phone.

An hour later (or so) saw us huddled in Milady's tower, us being me, Jay and Val. At that elevation, the air was stiflingly hot, even past midnight. Insufficient windows had a lot to do with that, and since its principal occupant must be impervious to either heat or cold, nobody bothered with incidental practicalities like trying to keep it at a habitable temperature. I sat wilting in the chair House had politely set for me (the thing bulged out of the wall in a gloriously grotesque display, if House ever gets tired of hosting the Society I think it has a career in horror films). Fanning oneself with one's own hand really doesn't achieve much, but you probably knew that.

Val looked as cool as ever, reclining at her ease in her poison-green chair. I was somewhat relieved to notice beads of sweat upon Jay's brow, and an appearance one might (if one were as ruthless as Val) term reminiscent of a "wrung-out dishcloth". In the face of Val's effortless cool, it was nice not to be the only person dripping all over the place.

Anyway.

Milady had heard our three-way report calmly, and fallen into one of her thoughtful silences. I'd had ample time to scrutinise both of my companions, plus the floor, the ceiling, the walls and the rose-damask upholstery of House's choice of chair (stylish, House, can I keep it?) before Milady finally spoke.

'Delicate,' she mused. 'I do not think I have encountered so thorny a problem in some time.'

'See?' I said, feeling vindicated. 'The way forward is by no means clear.'

'Oh, I believe it is,' said Milady.

All right, then.

'There can be no doubt that the mines must be investigated, if there is the smallest possibility that they might be able to furnish us with what we need. The modulator must be our priority.'

'Agreed,' I said, and Jay nodded.

'As a second point of some importance. Have any of you uncovered any concrete evidence that the Elvyng family is aware of Cicily's secret, and that they continue to exploit it?'

I had to think about that for a moment. So twisty and turny had been our path to this discovery, I'd forgotten what evidence we'd found — and which of our theories had been based wholly on speculation. 'There's Cicily's last will and testament,' I offered. 'When she "died", she certainly left all of her papers, including presumably any books, to her Elvyng son. And he probably inherited her enchanted portrait, too.'

'But,' said Jay, 'that may no longer be relevant. If Crystobel Elvyng was right, and Cicily had nothing to do with the argent in the end, then her personal papers aren't relevant now.'

'True.'

'And Mary Werewode may have left no books either,' said Val. 'Cicily's behaviour strongly suggests she communicated with her ancestress directly, or near enough. We previously assumed there must have been extant books or letters only because we were not yet aware of the painting issue.'

'The paintings are interesting,' said Milady. 'Jay, what do you know of those?'

Jay's knowledge had already been offered up as part of our report. He'd betrayed some small discomfort during that part of our narration, which I put down to a degree of guilt over having snooped through prohibited books. But at Milady's words, he cast a sideways glance at me, and shifted in his chair. 'I don't know what you mean,' he said, transparent as glass. 'I've already told you everything.'

'Come, Jay. This is important.'

Jay gave a tiny sigh. 'They teach it, at the academy. Only the theory, naturally there are no practicals. But they regard it as a functional art.'

'You didn't mention that before,' I said.

Hence the sideways glance — guilt at keeping secrets from me. He did it again. 'We were bound to the deepest secrecy,' he said. 'Such classes would certainly be closed down, if the Ministry got wind of them.'

'So you didn't stealth through the secret archives for forbidden books?' I felt obscurely disappointed.

Jay coughed. 'Well… I did that, too.'

'My hero.' I beamed.

'To be fair, every self-respecting Academy student did. I suspect the professors knew, too. A ruthless zeal for knowledge is kind of a prerequisite for attendance.'

'Makes one wonder about the other paintings at the academy, doesn't it?' said Val, wisely cutting in on this rambling sideline.

'Rather,' I agreed. 'I wonder if they have Mary's.'

'Returning to the question of evidence,' said Milady. 'Do you know them to possess any images of Mary Were-wode?'

'No,' I said.

'Anything else that might offer proof of their knowledge of her work?'

'No,' I said, but I was looking at Jay. So was Val. He was the only one of us who had any depth of knowledge about the academy, after all.

'Don't look at me,' he said, holding up his hands. 'I at-tended the academy, but that gives me zero special knowl-edge of the family, or any of their private doings.'

'Crystobel Elvyng's visit here is suggestive of some special interest in the subject of the argent,' I said. 'But that is not proof of prior knowledge, either. We know of no absolute reason why Cicily might have hidden something so important from her family-by-marriage, nor any absolute reason why she might have shared it. So in short, I don't think we have anything concrete.'

'In that case,' said Milady, 'I believe we will take a small gamble.'

'Small?' I echoed.

'If you are not too tired, I believe an excursion to the mines cannot be undertaken too soon.'

Excitement flared in my eager little heart, and I sat up, my heat-related sufferings forgotten. I hadn't truly expected Milady to give us the go-ahead to explore the mines. She had to navigate some delicate political waters, after all, and making an enemy of the Elvyng family could do the Society no good.

But she really, *really* wanted that modulator.

So did I.

18

'WHEN YOU SAY "SOON", do you mean "before Crystobel Elvyng could conceivably do anything else to impede us"?' I said.

'Precisely. If the Elvyngs possess such knowledge yet have not chosen to make it public, we can always employ the defence of ignorance. But not if we engage in the kind of delay that might lead to intentions becoming known, and measures taken to prevent unauthorised explorations or inconvenient discoveries.'

'The mines don't belong to them, after all,' I said. 'Presumably they are still the property of the Yllanfalen.'

'Whether they might have an agreement with Aylligranir, or are operating independently and without the queen's knowledge, might prove an interesting point,' agreed Milady. 'But not yet a relevant one.'

'Speaking of Aylligranir,' I said. 'Did they send the moonsilver that they promised?'

'It arrived,' said Milady. 'I am not sure what her majesty intended by it.'

'Why is that?'

'In itself, it is insignificant. The sample is only an inch wide, and unworked.'

'Unworked.' I drummed my fingers on the arm of my chair, thinking. 'Unworked. How much moonsilver, or argent, is left in the world, would you think?'

'All of it, surely,' said Jay. 'It cannot be destroyed, that we know of.'

'Yes — and the examples of it that we've seen or heard of have all been finished articles, or in other words, very much worked. How much *unworked* argent is likely to be left, hundreds of years after all the known mines ran empty?'

'Not... much,' said Jay.

'Exactly. So how does Aylligranir have even a small piece of the raw stuff?'

'Either they have a stash of the raw metal put by, and have somehow managed to preserve it into the twenty-first century,' said Jay. 'Or...'

'Or they have a source,' I finished. 'Like the mines. We gave her majesty a fairly comprehensive account of our purpose in seeking argent, Milady. I thought at the time that she was peculiarly uninterested and unhelpful, but perhaps I was wrong. Perhaps this unworked piece is a hint.'

'Why a hint?' said Jay. 'Why not just say, *oh, we happen to have a renewable source of exactly what you're looking for, why don't I send you a catalogue?*'

I shrugged. 'Is that what you would have done, in her shoes? Not everyone can be trusted, even those employed by the Society. We could have been anybody, with any motive. A likely story is proof of nothing.' I thought of Miranda as I spoke, and Ancestria Magicka. Her majesty of Aylligranir probably wasn't unwise to work around the subject, considering the extraordinary value — and power — of the substance in question.

'Take the argent with you,' said Milady, wisely skipping over the question entirely. I swear, one of these days I will drive myself mad with my wacky theories. 'House, if you would?'

The wall rippled. Something unspeakable oozed out of it and dribbled towards the floor, followed by a nugget of something pale silver and gleaming.

'I feel like House isn't a huge fan of summer,' I murmured.

'It is maintenance season,' said Milady. 'We've had builders in all week.'

'That would suck,' I agreed. Like a trip to a particularly aggressive beautician: unpleasant as a process, but the results would be worth it. Hopefully.

Val had scooped up the argent, and sat examining it, having cleaned the physical expression of House's displeasure off it with a tissue. 'It feels interesting,' she said, and passed it to me. 'I never saw it in its raw state before.'

The moment it touched my palm, I yelped, and dropped it. 'Ouch,' I hissed, shaking my hand to dislodge the pain. 'It burns, but like... ice.' The stuff had left a silvery, moon-coloured burn-mark on my skin, rather attractive if one forgot the pain that came with it. Which I wasn't.

Val stared at me, and held up her own hands. Both were unmarked. 'Sparking again, Ves?'

'I don't *think* so...' I stared balefully at the innocuous lump, lying there on the carpet all innocent-looking. 'Jay, you carry it.'

'Thanks,' he said dryly, but when he bent to pick it up, he emerged unscathed. The argent lay in his palm, meek and harmless.

'I can't tell if it passionately loves me or violently hates me,' I muttered.

Jay looked at me. 'Like the lyre.'

'The lyre is something else again.' I rose from my chair. 'We'd best get going. It's getting late.'

'One thing,' said Jay, following suit. 'We had enough trouble getting into Aylligranir before. How are we going to reach Everynden?'

'This is a problem I would be delighted to solve for you,' said Milady. 'Had I the means.'

In other words: good luck.

'Right,' said Jay, heading for the door. 'Back later, then.' He stopped. 'Wait. Val, can I raid the maps?'

'Don't leave them out of order.'

'Wouldn't dream of it.'

'So,' I said, shortly afterwards. 'How do you even do this? Can you only travel to henges you've been to, or that you know the location of?'

For some reason, Jay laughed. 'Sometimes I wish that was true, but no. It's quite possible to end up in a henge that probably hasn't been visited in living memory, and is marked on zero maps.'

I raised a brow in his general direction. 'And you know that how?'

He coughed. 'Let's say I've had a mishap or two in my time.'

We were down in the cellar, stationed in the centre of House's private henge, waiting while the Winds of the Ways curled their way up out of nothing. 'So you... what?' I prompted. 'Aim? Cross your fingers and hope for the best?'

'Something like that. If I know roughly where a henge is stationed, I can shoot for it. Doesn't always work out as intended.' His eyes had a faraway look, focused on whatever mysterious, arcane processes went on when Jay took to the Ways. 'The most recent map Val's got of Aylligranir is a couple of hundred years old, but henges and towns don't move about much, so it should be good enough. We're going back to the same henge we used before, that'll get us back to the entrance. Then there's a henge marked inside of Aylligranir, pretty close to Everynden.'

'Still doesn't get us past the border,' I pointed out. Even I knew that Waymastery didn't work into the Yllanfalen kingdoms. They'd blocked passage from outside henges long ago, whenever it was they decided they'd had about enough of the outside worlds.

'One problem at a time.'

No time for more, as the Winds reached howling potency and swept us away. I kept my face down, clinging to Jay, as we soared in a rush through a thousand miles — might as well have been — and came down in a cool, moonlit glade somewhere in the Dales.

Back, then, through the hills, a whole new landscape at this hour, scarcely recognisable as the same countryside we had trekked through only a day or two ago. The moon, nearing full, bathed everything in a pale, soothing glamour, and cast stark shadows behind every bush and tree. I breathed the cool air, savouring the balmy night winds, though we were still clammy with perspiration by the time we arrived back at the hillside that divided us from Aylligranir. No sunbathing today, nor moonbathing either. I felt a sense of suppressed urgency, as though time raced against us; if we did not find a way to Everynden now, *today*, this instant, some window of opportunity would close, some door slam in our faces, and it would all be over.

'Now what?' I said, pacing through the bone-dry grass. I eyed the darkened slope balefully, as though it had personally arrayed itself in our way.

'So,' said Jay, and to my puzzlement he sat down in the grass, cross-legged, and facing the emphatically closed door into Aylligranir. 'I told you my mother petitioned the Yllanfalen on my behalf, right?'

Giddy gods. For weeks I'd wished for story-time-with-Jay, to little avail, and *now* he wanted to get chatty? 'Yes,' I said dubiously. 'I recall.'

'Some of the kingdoms granted an audience, even if they didn't grant her request. And one time, she told me an interesting story.'

'The queen?'

'My mother. While she was there, she saw someone appear, apparently out of thin air, upon a wave of faerie music. Nobody would tell her how it was done. She thought the Yllanfalen had developed a way of transportation via music itself, but I think it might have been a bit different from that.'

'I hate to rush you, but could we skip to the relevant bit?'

'This is the relevant bit. I think that person was a Waymaster, using a sunk henge my mother couldn't see.'

'Uh huh. And the music?'

'Exactly. Was the music incidental, or was it an intrinsic part of the process?'

'Still not really seeing your point.'

'The henges inside the Yllanfalen kingdoms are only blocked to outsiders. Right? They have to be functional for the kingdom's own citizens, supposing they have Waymasters left to use them. So how is that accomplished? What twist of magick is required by Yllanfalen Waymasters to use those henges?'

'Musical?' I said, light dawning.

'Probably? Virtually everything they do involves music in some form or another. So, if we can find a way to blend Waymastery magick with Yllanfalen music-magick, maybe we can jump from here to the henge near Everynden.'

I released the hillside from my baleful scrutiny, and turned it upon Jay instead. 'And you didn't mention this two days ago because of why?' We'd spent hours failing to get in, and Jay had left *me* to figure out a way inside. While he napped.

'Did you know there's a book about the ethics and legalities of Waymastery? It's this thick.' Jay made a space about three inches wide with his fingers. 'One does not force one's way into blocked henges, especially if they're inside closed fae enclaves. It isn't a thing to be done lightly.'

'So why now, Mr. Play-by-the-rules?'

'Well,' said Jay. 'If Milady thinks this is worth a gamble, so do I.'

'I'll get you your Team Rulebreaker cap and badge tomorrow,' I promised.

'And I shall wear them proudly, at least for the thirty seconds or so before the Ministry shows up to arrest me.' He rose from his seat upon the grass, and advanced upon me. Considering enough of him was in shadow that I couldn't see his face, I found this somewhat intimidating.

I stepped back. 'So, um, what's my role in this delightfully crazy venture? You're the Waymaster, *and* the Yllanfalen musical talent.'

'And you're the one with the third ingredient that seems to be important in this context, that being moonsilver.'

'You've got the moonsilver. Or, I hope you do.'

Jay opened his palm. The nugget of raw argent glimmered there, like a bubble of moonlight. 'I meant your pipes.'

'Those are *skysilver* pipes, thank you. Can we please get our fanciful fae terminology right?'

'Whatever. Most of the Yllanfalen we met in your mother's kingdom had a set of pipes, whether moonsilver or not. Coincidence? And you've got a headful of Yllanfalen pop songs, to boot.'

'So you want me to play while you...' I waved a hand vaguely. 'Do whirly things?'

'Please.' He was still advancing.

I stepped back again. 'Jay, what are you doing.'

'I can't spirit you away out of thin air.'

'I thought that was exactly what you were going to do.'

'I do need to hang onto you. And since your hands are going to be busy, I guess you get a hug.'

'Oh.' I stopped retreating. 'Um, okay...' I tried not to feel weird as Jay's arm slid around my waist, and took a firm grip of my hip. In fairness, his thoughts were obviously far from the facts of physical me, for he was already calling up his whirly magicks; arcane winds stirred my hair.

I took out my pipes, and hesitated. What exactly was I meant to do? I wasn't a musical magician, not like the Yllanfalen. Or Jay. Any potency my modest musical efforts possessed came from the pipes, not from me. Surely that couldn't be enough, or any one of the incredibly few Waymasters left in Britain who happened to be in possession of a priceless set of ancient skysilver pipes could pop in and out whenever they liked...

Well, okay. This almost unthinkably rare confluence of circumstances did not constitute a grave security problem, now did it? No such person existed. Just me and Jay, Team Improbable.

I played. Not the lullaby. Was it one o'clock still, or two? Three? Fatigue plagued me but little yet, probably the effects of excitement and adrenalin. I felt it, though, weighing upon my limbs, slowing my thoughts. It wouldn't take much to convince my brain — and Jay's — that now would be a great time to fall asleep for eight hours or so. I skipped over the sprite-song, too, not wanting to attract Flow's notice at this time.

'Jay,' I said, breaking off playing. 'We're breaking and entering!'

'Keep playing,' he muttered.

I played a bit more. 'What, this isn't the jail-worthy kind so it's okay?'

'Something like that. *Keep playing.*'

Something was happening. Winds swirled, ice-cold and smelling, incongruously, of wet earth. My feet came off the floor, and suddenly I was grateful for Jay's grip on me, for

I felt untethered otherwise, like I might have flown away into the ether, never to be seen again.

'Nearly—' Jay gasped.

A bell tolled somewhere, a mournful sound that sent a chill down my half-frozen spine.

Then the half-frozen feeling spread to my feet, for suddenly I was up to my ankles in sodden mud, and the shadowed hillside was gone.

'I think,' said Jay, looking down at his own begrimed feet. 'I think we did it.'

I looked around, to no real effect. Tree-cover loomed over our heads, too night-darkened to determine details, and too thick to permit much more than an occasional beam of moonlight to filter down. I discerned the vague outline of a craggy block of stone somewhere near my left knee; a section of a henge?

'And that,' said Jay, releasing me and taking an experimental step, 'has to be absolutely the only time we ever do that.'

I snorted. 'Uh huh.'

'I'm serious. What we just did was not okay. We broke one fixed magickal law and contravened a slew of ethical agreements.'

I patted his shoulder. 'Milady won't let us go to prison.'

'I think you rely a bit too much on Milady's influence.'

'It's been working for me for ten years. Right, which way?'

'How should I know?' said Jay.

Oh, boy.

19

I T TOOK US TEN minutes to trudge our way through to a road, by the end of which time I had mud up to my knees and I couldn't feel my toes. 'Isn't it meant to be summer?' I groused, trying in vain to shake the cold, sludgy grime out of my sandals.

Jay made no answer. He glanced up and down the road, which was a beautiful construct of white stone. The tree-cover having thinned somewhat, it shone silver under the moon. 'I think this way,' he said, picking a direction at what looked to me like random.

Being Jay, though, he was perfectly right. Soon enough, the walls of a town appeared on the horizon, with clustered houses behind it. Built from the same white stone as the road, the town looked a creation of pure magick, like it had coalesced out of moonlight itself, and would vanish with the rising of the sun.

Hell, this was fairyland. For all I knew, that's exactly what it was.

'Hoping that's Everynden,' I said.

'The maps showed no other towns in the vicinity of that henge,' said Jay. 'Though being two hundred years out of date, who knows.'

'And the mines are where in relation to the town?'

'Somewhere around here,' said Jay, and fell over.

I ran to his side. 'Jay! Curse it, we should have something sensible out here, like lights.'

No answer. I searched the darkened ground for his prone form, and found nothing but empty air.

'Jay?'

He hadn't fallen over. He had disappeared.

'Jay!' I yelled. 'This is a bad habit of yours!'

'Sorry,' he said from behind me, and I leapt a foot or so in the air.

'And to think I used to *like* the night-time,' I said plaintively. 'Where did you go?'

All I could see of him was a tall, shadowed figure with threads of moonlight in his hair — and a glowing nugget of argent in the hand he held up. 'Remember Torvaston's tower?'

'It was only the other week.'

'And how the snuffbox worked?'

'Like a passport to his majesty's bedchamber.'

'I don't know if that's a passive property of this argent stuff, or only a popular use for it, but thanks to this burny nugget of argent I appear to have found the mines.' He held out a hand, which I tentatively took.

One step, two, and… three steps. Four. It took five or six before I realised we'd travelled from the grasslands outside Everynden into somewhere else. An underground somewhere, if the sudden, crisp chill in the air and the dampness against my bare arms was anything to go by.

'I wonder if her queenship knew it would do that,' I said.

'Conspiracy theory says yes,' said Jay.

'Top marks!'

Down below, even the moonlight failed us. We were entombed in the kind of utter darkness that blind, screaming panics are made of, and I engaged in a touch of unseemly haste as I summoned a little light-wisp to save us. White radiance flared. I sent the wisp floating high, and took a moment to collect myself as I looked around.

If you've ever visited natural cave formations, you'll have some idea of what we saw. It wasn't one of those vast, echoing kinds, the sort it would take half an hour to cross. Just a little one, with walls of mottled stone smoothed by endless years and the soft trickle of running water seeping in from somewhere above.

Here and there, deep holes had been hacked into the stone. Whatever had been removed from these jagged channels had left the faintest, silvery gleam behind, and my heart leapt.

'Look,' I said, trotting over to the nearest of these, and gingerly laying my hand against that silver tracery. It didn't burn me, not the way the pure argent had, but I felt a sharp *thrumming,* as of lingering potential. Memory? Magick? The argent may be gone, but it had left something of itself behind. Something Mary Werewode had learned to capitalise upon.

Jay began a circuit of the cave, the soft sounds of his footsteps drifting back to me. 'I don't see any new argent, er, growing, or whatever it does,' he reported.

'This can't be the entire mine, though,' I answered. 'Surely just a small part of it? And what about the moonlight?'

'I see I have guests,' said a new voice, and I once again jumped half out of my skin.

I whirled about, but saw no one. 'Who's there?'

'Can you not guess?' It was a woman's voice, pitched a little low, and perfectly composed. My eyes narrowed. I'd heard it before, and recently too.

'Ms. Elvyng?' I ventured.

She laughed, and came at last into view, traversing some hidden bend in the tunnels we had yet to discover. 'Sharp,' she said, smiling at me. 'Somehow I knew the two of you would be troublesome.'

I looked around for Jay, and found him drawing nearer to me. Unease prickled, and I despised the gut-dropping sense of uncertainty that briefly robbed me of all the sharp wits she had just praised. *This* we had not anticipated. What would she do? Was the argent a secret worth killing for?

She stopped a few feet before us, amusement still curving her lips and brightening her eyes. 'You look white,' she said to me. 'And braced for combat,' she added, looking then at Jay. 'Come now, you can hardly imagine I would harm you, and I hope you won't be so rude as to offer violence to me. The Society has better manners, no?'

'We *are* trespassing,' I pointed out.

'Yes, and I'd be inclined to escort you out. Only I cannot imagine how you could possibly have contrived to enter here without the queen's permission.'

'She didn't precisely give permission,' I admitted. 'But that's because she didn't tell us about this place. She did give us a... clue, however.'

Jay held up the nugget of argent. 'Which, as it turns out, was also an entry ticket.'

Crystobel Elvyng nodded. 'You know, the Society has a reputation for persistence. Wit. Expertise. To a degree frequently decried as highly inconvenient, and I find I now understand what they mean. It isn't precisely ideal that you've nosed your way into this particular secret.'

'We have good reason,' I said quickly.

'Which is what, exactly? I am afraid this partnership is not open to new members at this time.'

'Partnership?'

'The Yllanfalen own the mines. We own the secret of dredging new argent from within them. It is an arrangement which suits us both.'

'We have zero designs on your secrets.' It cost me to say that, for this was a secret I badly wanted to be let into. Who wouldn't? But the goal was not the process; it was the product we wanted.

'Just on the argent,' I added.

Crystobel Elvyng raised one elegant brow. 'I don't precisely follow.'

'If you have a supply of raw argent, we're buying,' Jay said.

'Well,' I amended. 'Most probably the Court at Mandridore will do most of the buying.'

Crystobel Elvyng looked from me to Jay and back again, no longer amused. A frown of mild puzzlement creased her brow. I noticed she wore heavy, protective gloves, and a collection of stoppered glass vials hung from a belt around her waist. She'd been working down here? 'Why don't you tell me exactly what it is you're trying to do?'

A LITTLE LATER, WE sat at our ease in an adjacent chamber, surrounded by glimmering chunks of the mysterious argent we'd spent so many weeks searching for. A break in the otherwise uninterrupted stone of the cavernous ceiling permitted a few stray beams of moonlight to filter down, and in the channel below, pale moonsilver formed in the rock walls.

I sat upon a low, smooth stone, Jay beside me, watching as Crystobel went through a range of incomprehensible motions involving the contents of those same vials. 'To be truthful,' she was saying. 'I don't precisely know how or why it works. None of us do, at this distance of time, for Mary stopped speaking to us long ago. I only know a certain range of motions that must be gone through, and conditions that must be maintained, in order to keep this process going. These,' she said, looking severely at me, 'we will not be sharing.'

'That's fine,' I said, though it wasn't. My scholar's heart, ever avaricious for secrets, ached for more information, and I knew Val would be spitting chips. 'But can you supply the project?'

'I can make no concrete promises. As you may be able to tell, the argent does not form quickly, nor in great quantities.'

'I don't know that we need masses of it,' I said. 'That's a question for Orlando.'

She didn't ask who Orlando was. Doubtless she knew him by reputation already. 'When I came to see you,' she said, glancing briefly at us, 'I had expected the Society would be open with me about its reasons for pursuing information about Cicily — and, as I suspected, my argent.'

'Fair,' I allowed.

'It's a sensitive project,' said Jay, when I said nothing else. 'We, um, haven't always known who we can trust with the full details.'

'There are those who would gladly co-opt the whole thing for their own gain,' I added, thinking very much of Fenella Beaumont as I spoke. She'd said as much, last time we had seen her. *Ancestria Magicka will be the ones to restore magick to Britain.*

'And you thought we might be just such a type?' said Crystobel.

'No. But we didn't know that you were not. And you know, we were hoping the most prominent magickal family in England might not be keeping the most important secret in magick all to themselves.'

She inclined her head, and stoppered the last of her vials. I'd strained my eyes trying to get a glimpse of their contents, but besides vague impressions of colour and an occasional glimmer of magick, I'd discerned nothing of use. 'I suppose my behaviour has been similarly suspicious towards you,' she allowed. 'Or I might have attempted a negotiation before. As it was, I could have no better idea of your motives than you had of mine.'

'The Society *could* be a collection of soulless, money-grubbing thieves,' I agreed.

'Some might say that it is,' said Jay.

True. Some might, indeed.

'But you say not?' said Crystobel.

'Emphatically not. We're the good guys.'

Crystobel gave a small smile. 'Well, then,' said she, stripping off her gloves. 'I believe I will have two conditions.'

I straightened, sensing a challenge. *Conditions.* That boded either excitingly or appallingly, depending on what kind of a woman Crystobel Elvyng really was. 'Oh?'

'It is impossible to do otherwise than support this particular of the Society's aims, and as such my family will supply your argentine needs — within reason — free of cost. *If* the following conditions are met.'

Free? I sat up even straighter. That either meant Crystobel was a woman of extraordinary generosity — in which case, I felt even guiltier for distrusting her so much before — *or*, she had one hell of a set of conditions for us.

'One,' she said. 'The Society will not publicise any part of this process. Indeed, I prefer that the world at large continues in utter ignorance that it even exists.'

An obvious enough request, and not *too* unreasonable. It would be better if such a secret wasn't left in the hands of a single family; that was hardly fair. But it wasn't our business to interfere in a private pact between the Elvyngs and the Yllanfalen. Besides, if (when?) we succeeded with our goal, these traces of argent would no longer be half so necessary. There'd be more than magick enough in Britain, for everything good and marvellous anyone might wish to do.

'Two,' she went on. 'I want Merlin's grimoire.'

'What?' I blurted.

She just looked at me.

'Merlin,' I repeated. 'Merlin's grimoire.'

'A reasonable trade, I think?'

'But,' I said, and stopped, my brain reeling. 'But—'

'There never *was* a Merlin,' said Jay. 'And therefore, there can be no Merlin's grimoire.'

'That is a debatable point.'

Jay and I, mutually thunderstruck, stared at Crystobel.

Jay recovered first. 'It's an impossible task.'

'Can't we just pay for the argent?' I pleaded. Even if it cost half the earth — which it would — that would be a more achievable price to pay than an impossible artefact.

'Money I can get,' said Crystobel. 'I do not especially need more.'

I got a grip. 'You must realise how crazy this sounds,' I said, and I wondered at myself, for was I not usually the one enthusiastically promoting the craziest of ideas? 'If you can offer us some proof that this artefact exists—'

'I know it exists,' said Crystobel calmly. 'My family used to own it.'

'Um,' I said.

'Used to?' prompted Jay.

'It was stolen from us. Four years ago. The police were never able to recover it.' She smiled when I opened my mouth to speak, and added, 'Yes, I can offer proof. There is a purchase receipt, my father's property, listing its acquisition at a private auction. I also possess some photographs of the piece, and copies of one or two pages, plus an official valuation of the book for insurance purposes.'

I'd run out of objections that ran along the lines of *but that's impossible.* 'Merlin,' I croaked. 'Cannot be.'

Crystobel shrugged one shoulder. 'Truthfully, I am less concerned with the precise identity of the book's author than I am with the contents. Whether or not it was penned by the *real* Merlin, or merely someone using the name, it is priceless and irreplaceable. Its contents are responsible for many of the magicks and wonders upon which our family depends, and I must have it back.'

'We aren't detectives,' said Jay bluntly. 'If the police couldn't get it back for you, why do you imagine we can?'

'Are you not?' was all Crystobel said. The pointed look she cast around the cave illustrated her thinking clearly enough: official detectives we might not be, but we had demonstrated a talent for digging up secrets. Even ancient ones.

I admit to feeling a flicker of excitement begin to unfurl. 'Listen,' I said. 'I give you fair warning. If we find this grimoire, we are going to read it.'

'There's no stopping her,' Jay agreed. 'I know. I've tried.'

Crystobel grinned. 'If you get me my book back, you're welcome to read it. And I'll give you all the argent you need.'

That settled it. I love her.

20

'Nancy Drew,' I breathed. 'I've read every single title there ever was.'

'So?' said Jay.

'Every Sherlock Holmes. Agatha Christie. All of them.'

'Reading detective stories doesn't make you a detective, Ves.'

'No. But it can make you *want* to be a detective, and suddenly I do.'

'Wish granted.'

'Cordelia Vesper, Book Detective.'

'You already have a job, had you forgotten?'

I ignored this.

'Merlin's Grimoire,' said Val. Upon our return Home, we'd gone first to Milady's tower, second to breakfast, and had then, inevitably, rattled down to the library. Jay had voted for a few hours' sleep first. Lightweight.

'Isn't it exciting?' I beamed.

Val looked monumentally unimpressed. 'It sounds like a fool's errand.'

'No!'

'Like Ms. Elvyng has no intention of parting with her hard-won and priceless argent, but instead of being so rude as to say so, she's sent us on a goose chase.'

'She has all that proof of the book's existence,' I objected, gesturing at the laptop sitting on the corner of her enormous desk. Crystobel had been prompt in sending everything over. Val's email was bristling with scanned paperwork.

'Could be faked.'

'That would be a lot of effort to go to just to avoid having to say no,' I said. 'Besides, when did she have time to prepare it? We only spoke to her a few hours ago.'

'Maybe she set up this whole thing. Maybe she knew you'd be on her tail, and prepared a red herring especially.'

'Val. Much as I respect a sound conspiracy theory, that's usually *my* province. *Your* job is good sense.'

Val's gaze flicked to Jay, then back to me. 'Do you have any idea how many impossible books I've gone hunting for?'

'Um. A few?' I hazarded.

'Quite a few. Books that somebody *swore* had existed, at one time or another. Books that could change everything, if only we could get a look at their contents. None of them ever worked out, Ves.'

And I saw the problem. Val had hoped, over and over again, and been disappointed. Some irrepressible part of her was hoping again; hoping that *this* incredible tome might be the one that was real. That it might have survived the destructive passage of centuries. That we might be able to reclaim it.

She didn't want to hope, because she didn't want the disappointment.

'How about this,' I said. 'We'll hope for the impossible things. You can go on being the Voice of Reason, or even the Voice of Crazy Conspiracy Theories. I'll step aside. I don't mind.'

'We might need a bit of help, though,' Jay said. 'That's why we're here.'

That won him a scowl. 'Right, ask the library lady, because she knows everything about all books known to man or beast. If I knew about *this* one, don't you think I would have moved heaven and earth to get it already?'

'Three weeks ago, we knew of no source of raw argent,' Jay said. 'Three months ago, we didn't even know argent existed.'

'What's your point?'

'Nothing's impossible.'

Val grunted.

'We get to read it, Val,' I said. 'Imagine.'

'I am imagining.' Sourly said.

'I promise to find it,' I said solemnly. 'And if I don't, you can have my crystal chest and all of its contents.'

'Including the regenerating tea cup?' said Val.

'Yes.'

'And the endless chocolate pot?'

I swallowed. 'Yes.'

Her eyes narrowed. 'Lies.'

'Truth. We need that argent, and I *want* a look at that book.'

She heaved a great sigh — and then set aside her objections in the twinkling of an eye. 'Right,' she said. 'Jay, you're on police duty. Get in touch. See if you can get them to send over any police reports they have on the theft. Pull Milady's influence if you have to.'

'But why would—' began Jay.

Val glared.

'Right.' He shot up from his chair, and left.

'Ves, media duty. News reports. Gossip pages. Obscure treatises upon the arcane. We'll need every reference to Merlin's Grimoire that's ever been made, especially any that intersect with mentions of the Elvyng family. Plus, if you find any mention of bad blood between the Elvyngs and any other family or group, highlight that too.'

'Yes, ma'am.' I got up from my chair. 'And what are you going to do?'

'Me? I'm going to deep dive into the magickal dark web.' Val stretched, cracked her knuckles, and opened up her laptop. 'Somebody had the gumption and the know-how to steal from the Elvyngs, *and* get away with it. I rather fear we're dealing with a considerable power.'

Also By Charlotte E. English

Modern Magick

The Road to Farringale

Toil and Trouble

The Striding Spire

The Fifth Britain

Royalty and Ruin

Music and Misadventure

The Wonders of Vale

The Heart of Hyndorin

Alchemy and Argent
The Magick of Merlin
Dancing and Disaster

223

House of Werth

Wyrde and Wayward
Wyrde and Wicked
Wyrde and Wild

9 789492 824356